HER MERCY

A RIVER REAPERS MC NOVELLA

ELIZABETH BARONE

ALSO BY ELIZABETH BARONE

STANDALONE NOVELS

Any Other Love

Crazy Comes in Threes

Just One More Minute

The Nanny with the Skull Tattoos

Sade on the Wall

The Stairs Between Us

RIVER REAPERS SERIES

A Disturbing Prospect

A Risky Prospect

Her Mercy (A River Reapers MC Novella)

SOUTH OF FOREVER SERIES

Twisted Broken Strings

Diving Into Him

Savannah's Song

What Happens on Tour

Visit **elizabethbaronebooks.com** to purchase!

MAIETTA INK

Her Mercy

A River Reapers MC Novella

Copyright © 2019 by Elizabeth Campbell, writing as Elizabeth Barone

All Rights Reserved

1st Edition

Cover photography by alexvolot and feedough | Depositphotos

Cover designed by Natasha Snow

ISBN 978-0-9912838-9-7

❀ Created with Vellum

HER MERCY

Twenty years ago, Mercy and Bree chose loyalty over love. Now they can do it all over—if he can find her.

War veteran Mercy has an ache in his bones that the MC he built with his best friend doesn't quite soothe. When beautiful runaway Bree shows up at the club house, both his physical and emotional pain begin to lift.

Despite their substantial age gap, Bree and Mercy find the home they've always been looking for in each other. But Bree is buckling under the weight of her own secrets, and they were never far behind her to begin with. When they catch up to her, she runs. Again.

When he finally catches up with her twenty years later, he's only got one shot to prove to her they belong together.

Her Mercy is a second chance romance that spans decades of heartache, and births the beginning of the River Reapers MC series.

This novella can be read as a standalone.

FOREWORD

I've wanted to write Bree's story ever since she walked onto the pages of *A Disturbing Prospect*. Man, is she a complicated character; at first, I hated her. I couldn't understand why she abandoned Olivia. The more I got to know her, though, the more I grew to understand and love her. Turns out we have something in common: we both survived rape.

And Mercy—oh, my sweet Mercy! I poured a lot of my own experience into him, too, drawing from my longtime battle with chronic pain.

As with all of the books in this series, some of the themes in *Her Mercy* may make some people uncomfortable, and maybe even be triggering for survivors of trauma. I have included a list of potential trigger and content warnings.

For the sake of realism, I've depicted biker culture from my own experience and understanding. Although that culture and its attitudes toward women is changing, it has a long way to go. My goal for this book and its subsequent series is to help change that mentality.

TRIGGER WARNINGS

Although I purposely wrote *Her Mercy* to be a bit less dark than *A Disturbing Prospect* and *A Risky Prospect*, it still contains some themes that might be uncomfortable or even triggering for some readers. As a rape survivor, I am a huge supporter of trigger warnings in entertainment; I cannot tell you how many seemingly fluffy romances I picked up, only to find themes I wasn't mentally prepared for. When you have PTSD or something else you struggle with, being equipped is an essential tool in your recovery.

Here are the potential trauma triggers, as well as a content warning.

- **Age Gap Romance:** There is a substantial age difference between Bree and Mercy; she is 14 and he is 33 when this book begins.
- **Drug and Alcohol Use:** Some characters use drugs and drink alcohol.
- **Childhood Sexual Assault:** Several characters have a history of being molested as children.
- **Guns and Violence:** My vigilante bikers use guns to

fight the bad guys, as well as other violent means of taking out the trash.

- **PTSD from Rape:** A character experiences flashbacks, anxiety, and other symptoms of PTSD due to being raped by a teacher. Most of this is mentioned vaguely, on purpose; I needed to write a bit of a lighter book after *A Risky Prospect*.

If you feel that you won't be safe reading *Her Mercy*, please don't risk your health. As a rape survivor and someone with PTSD, I wish many books came with a list of trigger warnings. No book is worth your well-being.

Please also note that I don't necessarily condone or endorse the themes contained in this book. I do, however, wish it was legal to kill rapists.

If you've read *Her Mercy* and feel that I may have missed something, please email me at elizabethbaronebooks@gmail.com.

PART I

THE DRIFTER

1

NOW

I breathe a sigh of relief as the train pulls out of the station. He didn't come after me. I didn't really expect him to, considering I kind of just dropped that bomb on him and walked away. Typical me. Still, there was a slim chance he'd chase me, but he didn't.

No one is chasing me now.

I lean back against the seat and watch through the window as New Haven, Connecticut fades away. It occurs to me that I don't *really* have a reason to run. Ravage thought it might be best until things cool off, but I could've told him to go fuck himself. Instead, I took his money and let his Prospect collect me and drop me off.

It doesn't take a psychoanalyst to figure out why I keep running from this state.

By now I should be tired of running. The truth is, I find it thrilling. Leaving not only gives me a clean slate, but also an opportunity. There are fifty states in this country and millions of people—ample places and faces to get to know.

I always end up back here.

Not this time.

This time will be different.

This time, I'll stay away.

* * *

The train rolls into Norfolk, Virginia thirteen hours later. The conductor on the loudspeaker pronounces it "No Fuck," informing us that this is the last stop. I peer out the window, scanning the dusty parking lot for my ride and new roommate. There are too many people milling around, so I grab my bag and get off the train.

I step to the side so I'm not blocking the other passengers getting off and shield my eyes with a hand. I wish I'd thought to grab his sunglasses. They were some silly designer frames, but they'd come in handy right about now.

I've got no idea what this woman is supposed to look like, and I don't have a cell phone, either. If she doesn't show, I'll have to figure something else out. I don't panic because I always do.

"Bree?"

I wrinkle my nose at the woman in front of me. "You've got to be kidding me."

"I never kid around." She winks.

Same old Claudine, with the word *Cunt* tattooed down between her tits, her dark hair streaked through with red. "I must've got off the wrong stop," I mutter, turning back toward the train.

Somewhere in Connecticut, Ravage is laughing his ass off.

"Oh, come on, Bree. It's all water under the bridge." She grabs my bag, spinning me around. "Besides, you look beat. And hungry. You always got bitchy when you haven't eaten."

"I'm even more bitchy when you're around." I smooth my paisley skirt across my thighs. It's threadbare, but I'll wear it 'til it dies.

"So let's even you out, then. You look like you could use a burger. Three, maybe." She eyes the way my skirt hangs on my hips, how my ankles barely fill my boots.

I sigh. I *am* hungry. There's nowhere else for me to go, anyway, at least not right now. "Fine," I relent, "but you're buying."

I follow her to a beat up Subaru, watching her bony ass in that tight little skirt. I can't believe Ravage shacked me up with *her*. I'd just as soon be on the streets again. Which is probably where I'll go, the second my stomach is full.

I expect her to take me to a restaurant, somewhere I can just slip out when we're done. Instead, she drives the half hour to Hampton, where she pulls into a cute condo complex.

"Home sweet home," she sings.

I flinch. This can't possibly be *her* place. It looks so normal. I glare at the townhouse, crossing my arms.

"Oh, stop. Some of us get our lives together. Even a back-warmer like me." She pushes open the driver's side door and gets out, grabbing my bag from the backseat. Without another word, she marches inside, leaving the front door open.

Backwarmer. I sniff. More like homewrecker.

My stomach growls, reminding me what I came here for. As soon as I finish eating, I'm out of here. I follow her in, closing the door behind me out of habit. Immediately I wish I'd left it open. It's too loud in here, the walls painted an angry red. Blue armchairs, accent tables, and a coffee table try to anchor it, but the red and purple throw rugs only amplify it. Scarves in reds, blues, and purples cover the wall behind the blue couch.

I rub my temples.

The outside might look normal, but the interior looks like Claudine threw up everywhere.

I wrap my arms around myself, longing for the eggshell walls of state housing.

The kitchen isn't much better. The walls are still red, accented with more blue and a little golden yellow along the backsplash. I climb onto a stool at the counter dividing the kitchen from the dining area, and wrap my legs around its rungs.

Claudine dances around the kitchen, singing Bon Jovi while

cooking. Another reason I hate her, but not *the* reason. She puts a plate of three cheeseburgers down in front of me, then sits across from me, her placemat empty. She folds her hands.

I pick up a burger, and grease drips between my fingers. The sensation makes me want to wipe my hands, but there's no napkin holder on the table. I sink my teeth into the bun. Spices flood my senses, my mouth watering around the food. It's good.

Fucking Claudine.

Of *course* she can cook.

While I'm chewing my second bite, she leans forward.

"What?" I ask with my mouth full. She doesn't deserve manners, even if this might be the best burger I've ever had.

"I thought you'd wanna know," she begins, her eyes intent on mine.

I take another bite, mostly so I don't have to answer her. Almost one burger down. Two to go. Then I can go, too.

"Mercy's getting out," she says, and just like that, my day is ruined.

2

1997

I couldn't stomach the thought of telling anyone, so I ran.

I didn't go far. I was only fourteen, after all. I had no money, aside from the babysitting cash I blew on the bus hop out of Wolcott. I had no job experience, aside from babysitting a few kids on my street. And I had no high school diploma—a recent development.

I stood on the long strip of roads that made up Route 63 in Naugatuck, the bus pulling away from the curb and leaving me in a cloud of dust. I was officially out of cash—and adrenaline.

Glancing up and down the street, I looked for a sign, anything to tell me what to do next. I could go home. All I had to do was find a payphone and call my parents. Then I'd have to tell them why I'd run.

Nausea scraped against my stomach, clawing up my throat. I wrapped my arms around myself, pushing back against it and the memories. I couldn't tell them. No one would even believe me.

I started walking.

As I walked, I rubbed my hands up and down my arms. I hadn't even grabbed a coat on my way out, and it was freakin'

January. Not like I'd really had time to think things through. I stumbled into a parking lot, not even bothering to see what it was for. I just wanted to get inside and get warm. As I hurried toward the door, the backpack I wore slung on one shoulder brushed one of the motorcycles lined up out front.

"Hold it!" a gruff voice called out.

I froze in my tracks.

"Where do you think you're going?" he asked, stepping in front of me. He all but blocked out the sun—if the sun had been shining. The sky was a cold milk white.

I tipped my head back to look at him. The breeze ruffled the dark hair that just about covered his ears.

"You can't go in there," he continued, but all I saw were his lips. Thick, round lips that hugged every word he spoke. A constellation of stubble framed them, all that black facial hair only highlighting the pink plumpness of those lips. Shadows hung under his hypnotic brown eyes, more hair hanging in front of them.

I blinked, shaking myself out of my daze. A gust of wind whipped my hair into my face. I grabbed the dark strands, tucking them back into my shirt. "Why not?" I said between shivers. I glanced at the door again. It was so close.

"Because that," he said, jerking a thumb toward the building, "is a strip club. And *you* are like twelve."

I scoffed. "Eighteen."

"Same freakin' difference." He crossed his arms. "Shouldn't you be in school?"

Flicking my eyes from his face to the motorcycle, I crossed my arms, too. "Shouldn't you be in jail?"

"Probably." He laughed, and the sound flooded me with warmth—a heat so real, my fingers tingled.

"Move out of my way." I hopped from foot to foot. Ordinarily I'd never speak to an adult like that. And he was very much a man, probably in his early thirties. But I was freezing, and I had to pee. In about two minutes, I was going to be warm for a whole two seconds before I caught pneumonia.

"I can't let you in." He dropped the smirk, eyes warming a little. "Why don't I give you a ride home?"

I lifted an eyebrow at the bikes.

"In my truck." He jerked a thumb toward a pickup parked at the end of the line.

"So you're not a biker?" I had no idea why the question popped out. I was *cold*. I should've been climbing into the cab and blasting the heat as high as it'd go. Maybe I was just trying to delay going home. Or maybe I was disappointed that he wasn't a biker.

"That one's mine." He smiled proudly at one of the bikes. "If I put you on the back of that, you'll turn into an icicle. Come on. Where do you live?"

The door opened and a curvy woman with long blonde hair and bangs poked her head out. "Mercy! What the hell are you doing out here? Ravage and Bastard are at it again." She slipped back inside as quickly as she popped out.

He darted in after her, not even sparing a second glance at me. I counted to twenty, then opened the door.

The Guess Who's "American Woman" blasted over speakers I couldn't see in the dim light. What I could see, very clearly, was the woman spinning around a silver pole on a stage.

A strip club.

I almost laughed, but a hard body slammed into mine. He glared at me with green eyes before turning toward another man.

"We voted on this, Bastard! Split table means no escort service. You can't just do whatever the fuck you want!" the other man growled. His ice blue eyes nearly glowed with rage, his black hair damp.

Bastard launched himself at the other man. "The hell I can't. I built this goddamn business, Ravage!"

The man from outside—Mercy—shoved himself between them. "Enough!" he shouted, his voice rising even over the music.

Everything stopped. The girls dancing on stage edged out of the spotlight. The crowd of men with dollar bills in their hands stared at the trio in the middle of the floor.

"I'm not gonna abide this shit," Ravage said.

"Ravage," Mercy warned. "This is a club. We have to take this to the table, not the middle of the floor."

Bastard spat a wad of blood onto the floor. "Good call, VP." He sneered at Ravage.

Mercy's face hardened, then slipped back into a neutral mask. He clasped Ravage's shoulder. "Take a walk."

Fists curled, Ravage stalked outside, his blue eyes cold and unforgiving.

Mercy rose his voice again. "Show's over. Eyes back on the stage." He put an arm around Bastard and guided him to a door on the other side of the bar. They disappeared into the darkness.

"What are you doing in here, sweetie?" the woman from outside asked, spinning me around. Her blonde bangs framed anxious round eyes. Up close, I could see that they were brown instead of the usual blue. Outside, she'd looked angry, but inside she looked worried. It probably had less to do with me and more to do with the men.

"I was cold," I admitted, the first truth I'd spoken that day.

"It *is* pretty cold out," she said, steering me toward the door, "but you're too young to be in here."

"I'm eighteen," I blurted. "Are you hiring?"

She halted, looking me in the eyes. "I'm Shannon," she said, "and there's no way in hell you're dancing on that stage."

I swallowed. "Please," I begged. "I've got nowhere else to go."

She closed her eyes for a moment, her chest rising and falling. "Why do I always take in strays?" she muttered. Opening her eyes, she fixed them on me. "I'll figure something out for you. You're *not* dancing. Want a cup of hot cocoa?"

"Coffee, please." I licked my lips.

"Cream and sugar?" she asked as she stepped behind the bar.

"Black."

It was the second lie I'd told.

3

NOW

"Don't you at least want to see him?" Claudine calls after me.

I march toward the front door, bag in hand. I should've known this was all a setup. If I had a phone, I'd tell Ravage exactly what I think about all of this. I put my hand on the doorknob and turn it.

Claudine slips between the door and me, blocking my way out. Her chest heaves, her *Cunt* tattoo practically staring me in the face. "Don't you want to see your daughter? Don't you want your family back?"

I laugh. "Since when do you care about my family?" I spit the words at her.

She blanches, sagging against the door. "Water under the bridge," she says weakly.

"Yes," I say. "It's all over and done. Now let me through."

"I've been told . . . not to."

"By who? Ravage?"

She purses her lips.

"Claudine, you *owe* me this. Get out of my way."

"I've got a guest bedroom," she says. "There's your own bathroom. You'll hardly even notice I'm here."

I don't want to be *here*. Why Claudine is even still involved with the club is beyond me. She was all but banished after everything. Goddamn Ravage and his meddling.

I turn away, fuming. I never should've come to him and the club for help. I should've known there'd be a price to pay. There always is.

"Please," Claudine begs. "We both know I can't keep you here. I'm a heavy sleeper."

I roll my eyes. I don't want to know how she sleeps. Seeing her in bed with my husband was enough. I don't need any other visuals.

"Mercy wants—"

"I don't care what he wants," I tell her, shoulders sagging. The long train ride is finally catching up to me. "All I want is a hot shower and a good night of sleep."

"I can give you that," she says.

I march toward the stairs.

"It's the bedroom on the left."

I begin to climb.

* * *

Claudine's hot water isn't half bad. I stand under the stream for an hour before it runs cold. Her guest bed isn't bad, either. The sheets are clean and smell like Tide and Gain. How this homewrecking whore can afford the good shit is beyond me. There's a small dresser with an even smaller TV on top of it. I change my clothes and put everything back in my bag, then stretch out across the bed with the remote in my hand.

She's even got a decent cable package, with HBO and Showtime.

Goddamn Claudine.

I should've asked when he's supposed to be getting out. I have no idea how much time I've got.

I've got no plan, either.

What else is new?

Goddamn Mercy.

I put on a Lifetime movie and try to follow the plot: some woman stealing some other woman's baby. It's always the same, but I'm a sucker for these movies. I love the thrill, the not-so-surprising twist, the happy but ominous ending. I fall asleep halfway through, my dreams a tumble of brown eyes and big hands, golden wedding rings falling through the dark, a baby's cry.

When I wake, it's just a little after 7:00 a.m. The house is empty, but I find the coffee pot set up for me and a note from Claudine.

Have a good day.

I crumple it up and throw it in the garbage.

While the coffeemaker does its thing, I sit down at Claudine's table and try to figure out my next move. I can either sit around here and wait for her to get home—or even worse, for *him* to show up—or I can make my escape plan.

Shannon and Ravage gave me a little cash, and I have a bit more in my checking account from the waitressing job I had. That's one downside to being a drifter: a resume shot full of holes. I didn't even give them my two weeks' notice.

I've got enough for a couple nights in a motel or a couple more train tickets. Not both.

That's never bothered me, though. The universe has a way of arranging things for you, if you're prepared to take the leap of faith. I don't really know what I've got faith in anymore, other than my own two feet.

I find Claudine's laptop and turn it on, then make myself a cup of coffee while I wait for it to boot up. Her mugs are tiny, an insult to coffee and tea drinkers everywhere.

While I sip, I look up train schedules. My biggest hurdle is getting to the train station itself. After that, I can go anywhere:

down to Florida (always a good time), out to Colorado (even colder than Connecticut this time of year, but beautiful), even up to Canada (I think my passport is still good).

I'm weighing my options, making up my mind when someone knocks at the door.

4

1997

I made my way from the bar toward the stage, balancing a tray of drinks. As I passed a cluster of tables, someone grabbed my ass. I jumped back, the drinks spilling, my clothing instantly soaked.

I gaped at him, a gray-haired man with a dingy trucker's hat.

"Watch where you're going, sweet cheeks!" he bellowed in my face.

Glancing around, I tried to find Shannon. She stood behind the bar, her back turned to me as she mixed drinks. The music was too loud, the club too dark.

"You know the rules, Mac," a familiar voice growled. "Hands off our girls."

I swallowed. Mercy stood right behind me, the heat from his body burning into mine.

"Aw, I didn't mean nothing by it," Mac grumbled. "I'm just drunk."

"No excuses. Now get out."

"Come on," Mac slurred.

Mercy seized him by the collar of his stained T-shirt and

hauled him onto his feet. "I asked nicely," he said. "Don't make me ask again."

With a sneer, the old man lurched out of the bar.

I bowed my head, eyeing my wet clothes. I sighed.

Mercy lifted the tray from my hand, setting it onto a table. "Come on," he said without looking at me. "I'll show you where we keep the spare uniforms."

I followed him to a back storage room that held mostly booze. A rack of linens stood against the wall next to the door, though.

"Eighteen, huh?" he commented as he searched through the stacks of aprons and shirts.

I lifted my chin. "Yes."

"What in the world are you doing here? You and I both know you don't belong." He handed me a fresh black dress.

"How did you know my size?" I countered, checking the tag. He was dead on.

"What are you running from?"

I peeked up at him from between my lashes. "What makes you think I'm running?"

"So you really just want to get into the half-naked hospitality business."

I shrugged. "Why? Does it bother you?"

He used a hand to push his hair back from his face. "It bothers me because Shannon is good people. If you bring anything nasty to her doorstep, then you're hurting one of the last good people on this Earth."

Rolling my eyes, I edged toward the door. "Think whatever you want."

"You're the worst cocktail waitress I've ever seen."

"I'm sure you've seen a lot here," I shot back. "I'm going to get changed."

He spread his hands, his lips tipping in a crooked grin. "No one's stopping you."

"Great." Turning, I yanked open the door and stepped into the

cool, dark hall. Instantly my shoulders relaxed a little. I appreciated him kicking out that dirty old man, but the last thing I
needed was him asking more questions about me. Shannon
hadn't asked for ID or anything. Half the girls here were probably
runaways. I doubted *all* of the dancers were of age.

I hurried to the bathroom, where I stripped out of my soaked
clothing and shimmied into the fresh dress. All of the cocktail
waitresses at The Wet Mermaid wore the same low-cut black
dresses and stilettos. It was only my first week and I was about
one step away from breaking my neck.

But the pay was decent, and Shannon let me stay in a room
above the club.

"It's only temporary," she said with a warm smile, "considering
it's technically breaking the rules."

I wondered what rules she was talking about, but didn't ask. I
didn't ask much at all, to be honest. I just did as I was told,
grateful for the job and roof over my head.

Until Mercy had to start guilt-tripping me.

Why did he even care how old I was? I wasn't hurting anyone.
If anything, I was an extra pair of hands at half the pay rate.

I stepped out of the bathroom, tossing my soiled clothing into
the laundry bin. I tucked my wet panties into the pocket of my
apron, too embarrassed to add them to the business's laundry.

It was going to be an uncomfortable night.

"So where are you from, eighteen-year-old Bree?" Mercy
asked, stepping out of the storage room.

"Goddamn," I scolded him. "What do you, have a camera
on me?"

"Nah," he drawled. "Just impeccable timing." His round,
depthless brown eyes searched my face. "Me, I've lived here my
whole life."

"I didn't ask." I glanced at the end of the hallway. Sooner or
later, Shannon would notice I was missing.

"But I did." He grinned again. On any other man, it would've looked sly. On him, it looked boyish, mischievous. Maybe a *little* sly, but in a totally harmless, kind of sexy way.

"I'm from Connecticut," I hedged.

"Waterbury? No one ever likes admitting they're from Waterbury." He chuckled.

"Got me." I shrugged. "I've got to get back." I strode back toward the bar, not sparing him another glance.

"See you around, Bree from the Dirty Water," he called after me.

Throwing a hand over my shoulder, I flipped him off and kept walking.

5

NOW

The knocking continues, even though I'm standing between the kitchen and living room, eyes squeezed shut. As if that'll make him go away.

There's not enough time to run upstairs, grab my shit, and slip out the back door. I consider leaving it all behind, but then I'd have nothing. I've started from zero before, over and over again. Doesn't make it any easier.

It'd be easier than facing him after all this time.

I take a step toward the back door, praying it doesn't lead onto some weird enclosed porch. That'd be just my luck.

"Claudine!" hollers the knocker, who sounds like she's gargling cigarette smoke.

I tip my head back, relieved. It's not Mercy. I don't have to run.

Not yet, anyway.

I peer through the peephole and find a woman who can't be taller than four and a half feet. Her dishwater blonde hair is set in curlers, which shake as her fist begins beating on the door again.

"You can't hide from me, Claudine!" She kicks the door. It shudders in its frame.

She's strong, for such a little thing.

I don't really feel like dealing with her—or anyone, really—but it *would* be kind of fun to leave Claudine some kind of parting gift. I decide to see what this woman wants, and fling the door open.

Her fist freezes midair. "*You're* not Claudine," she says, voice accusing.

I glance down at my chest, then raise my eyes to her face pointedly.

"Where's Claudine?" She peers past me into the living room, as if Claudine is hiding behind the couch.

"She's . . ." It dawns on me that I have no idea where she is. Neither does her number one fan, apparently. "She's out. Maybe I can help you."

"Doubt it." She shakes her head, a curler precariously close to tumbling loose. "That bitch owes me money."

"For what?"

"Don't you sass me." She frowns, further wrinkling her already leathery face. "Oh, fine, she owes the HOA money, but *I'm* the treasurer. She can't avoid me forever!"

I bite my lip to hide the smirk. Claudine's behind on her condo fees—I've found the chink in her sleazy armor.

"I'm so sorry," I say. "She didn't tell you?"

"Tell me what?"

I glance around and lower my voice. "She's looking at another townhouse."

The treasurer gasps, her lip curling. "She isn't looking at Covenant, is she?"

This is too easy. These bitches are just as trigger happy as the officers in a motorcycle club, if not more. They're certainly cattier.

I spread my hands apologetically. "I'm afraid so. She said something about lower HOA fees."

Pinching her face, she turns on her heel and marches away. I can practically see the cartoon fumes coming out of her ears.

Smiling, I close the door and lean against it. That was fun, but probably not very nice of me. Still, the thought of Claudine getting an earful from this woman warms my cold soul and stifles any guilt.

Besides, I'm pretty sure Claudine will have no problem setting her straight. Our history aside, I've got to give her credit where credit's due. And Claudine can certainly hold her own.

I tamp down the spark of admiration. I refuse to respect the woman who destroyed my family.

Not that there was much of a family to begin with.

6

1997

"She's got nowhere else to go," Shannon hissed.

I stood behind the bar, drying and putting away highball glasses. The Wet Mermaid wasn't open yet—my favorite time of day. That was the only time of day the place was clean, both figuratively and literally.

"She ain't a member," Bastard seethed. "She ain't even somebody's ol' lady. She's just another one of your charity cases."

Cheeks hot, I kept my eyes on my task, pretending I couldn't hear them. It was hard not to when they were right in the hall.

"You better watch your mouth," Shannon snapped. "Remember who you're talking to."

"Who I'm talking to?" He laughed, a cruel grating that sent chills down my spine. "You better remember your place."

"My *place* is Sergeant-at-Arms' ol' lady," she shot back. "I'm also the one who keeps this place running, if you remember correctly."

A slap resounded through the bar. I flinched. The glass I'd been drying slipped from my fingers. I watched it tumble to the floor in slow motion. It spun toward the non-slip rubber mat, light glinting off the glass. It bounced off the mat, knocked into the cooler door, then fell onto the mat. It rolled toward the tile.

A black combat boot stuck out, stopping the glass. I followed the large boot, tracing the muscular leg clad in black denim, up, up the torso wrapped in a plain white T-shirt that hugged the abs. My gaze landed on his face, his watchful eyes.

"Th-thanks," I stuttered, cheeks flushing again. I squeezed my eyes shut. I wanted to be strong, like Shannon. Instead I always scampered around the club like a real mouse, avoiding the gazes of any of the MC members and doing everything I was told, whether it was sweeping or cleaning out the fryers.

And let Shannon take a beating for me, apparently.

Mercy bent to pick up the glass and I bent too, control of my limbs returning. Our hands reached for it at the same time, skin brushing skin. The second his warm hand touched mine, my nerves tingled, body going momentarily limp. His eyes snapped to mine, shock reflected in them.

He'd felt it too.

"Sorry," I mumbled, grabbing the glass and standing. I put my back to him. Even though I stood on both feet, my head spun. I peeked over my shoulder at him, but he no longer stood at the bar.

His voice floated from the hallway. I couldn't pick up what he said, but his soothing tone enveloped me. A moment later, he emerged with an arm around Shannon. A red splotch marred her fair skin, her eyes shining with angry tears.

"Ravage is gonna kill him," she hissed. There wasn't even a hint of regret in her words.

"I'll handle it." He lifted a finger to her cheek, tracing the red mark. "Are you all right?"

"I'm fine." Turning toward me, she sighed.

Mercy followed her gaze.

I swallowed, my cheeks flushing again. I forced myself to look at Shannon.

"How much of that did you hear?" she asked.

I put down the glass and towel. "I'll go. I don't want to cause any trouble."

Shannon's nostrils flared. "*You* didn't do anything wrong. And you're a damn good worker."

"Even with the occasional glass dropping." Mercy winked, and I felt warm all the way down to my toes.

"Truly, Bree. I can't keep a cocktail waitress. Bastard scares them all away."

Mercy raked his hair back from his face, pacing the length of the bar.

I bit my lip.

"Don't worry about Bastard, sweetie," Shannon assured me, coming around the back of the bar. She rubbed my shoulder. "We'll figure out another place for you to stay."

I blinked back tears. She was too kind. Mercy was too kind. If they knew the truth, they'd never be so warm and welcoming. I inched toward the hall, trying to come up with an excuse to go up to my room. "I'll be right back."

Shannon and Mercy exchanged glances.

"I don't think it's a good idea for you to go up there right now," she said softly.

Mercy's eyes flashed. "He's my best friend," he muttered, "but I've got no idea who he is anymore."

I frowned. Best friends? I'd only been around for a week, but as far as I could see, they had nothing in common. Except maybe the MC.

"Don't worry," Shannon said, giving me a smile that was supposed to be reassuring but didn't quite make it. "We'll figure something out."

I hung my head, eyes glued to the floor. I didn't want them to have to figure anything out. I'd gotten myself into the mess. I needed to pack my shit and get out of their lives. I had no business hanging around a bunch of bikers, anyway. Even if they'd treated me like family from the moment I started working.

All of them except for Bastard.

I thought it'd been some tough biker President act, up until the moment he hit Shannon. She was nothing but kind to everyone. In a way, she was sort of the glue that kept everyone and everything together and running. It shouldn't have surprised me, considering everything I'd heard about bikers was bad, bad, bad. But the other men never even raised their voices toward the women of the club.

The creep who'd grabbed my ass didn't count—he wasn't one of the River Reapers.

Still, they were bikers, and I didn't belong. I chewed my lip, panicking. I knew I should leave, but I didn't have anywhere else to go.

"She can stay in my room," Mercy said.

My head snapped up. "What?"

"You know what he'll say," Shannon said.

"It's my room. I can do whatever I want with it." He sat on one of the stools at the bar. At least he'd finally stopped pacing. All of that movement was making me nervous. He was so pent up, as if any moment he'd rush upstairs and throw a fist at Bastard.

"And he's going to tell you it's a club room." Shannon sighed. She scooped ice into a shaker, then added blackberry brandy. "Don't make this your problem. You've got enough on your hands."

She meant me, like I was a piece of furniture that needed to be stored somewhere. I cleared my throat. "*This* really isn't either of your problem. I'm sorry I caused so much trouble, but I can find somewhere else."

They exchanged glances again, and I wondered how long they'd been talking about me behind my back. I knew how it looked; a young woman with nothing but the clothes on her back begging for a job was obviously running away from something.

Still, I wasn't anyone's project. I didn't need them to conspire and treat me like a child.

I'd figure something out.

"What if," Mercy began, as if I hadn't spoken, "she's my ol' lady?"

Shannon laughed. "Do you really expect anyone to buy that? You haven't so much as kissed anyone in, God . . ." He voice trailed off, her gaze softening. She poured two shots of the brandy and pushed one toward him. "Besides," she asked him, with a glance at me, "how do you know Bree even wants to be your fake ol' lady?"

I willed myself not to blush and picked up the towel again. The glasses were dry, but I needed something to do with my hands.

"I can sleep somewhere else," he pressed. "I hardly ever sleep up there, anyway."

"You hardly ever sleep." She laid a hand over his. They both knocked back their shots, almost in sync.

I looked at them more closely. They had the same warm brown eyes. Somehow I'd missed it before. No wonder he was so pissed.

"I'm more concerned about your face." He set his empty shot glass down on the bar, the glass knocking against the wood.

"I'm fine," she said. "He's lucky I didn't kick him in the dick. I don't know if Ravage will have the same restraint. You need to handle this carefully, Merce. Things are tense enough."

He turned to me. "What do you say, Bree? Wanna be my fake ol' lady? I'll be a perfect gentlemen. The room's yours, if you want it."

I should've declined. I should've packed up the few belongings I'd accumulated in the past week and hightailed it out of there. Maybe things would've been completely different.

To make up for my prank, I do Claudine's laundry. Granted, I had some of my own. I bring one of my T-shirts to my nose, inhaling the clean scent of Tide and Gain. I've been washing everything by hand in whatever sink I can find for so long, it feels good to have truly clean clothes.

Around 3:30 in the afternoon, Claudine comes home.

"You're still here," she says, clapping her hands together. She's wearing Winnie the Pooh scrubs. A badge clipped to her shirt announces her as a nurse.

It's been such a weird day.

I say nothing from my perch on the couch. Instead, I sip from my tiny mug of tea. She's got the good stuff—a nice array of teas from all over the world. Who would've thought?

Her eyes sweep the neatly folded clothing on the coffee table. "You did my laundry?"

"I didn't know where everything went." It's a half truth. I just didn't want to set foot in her bedroom.

"Does this mean you're staying?" she asks, her tone tentative but hopeful.

"For tonight," I respond.

"You know," she says, setting down her bag and joining me on the couch, "I can get you a job at the hospital. We're always short on porters."

I take a sip of my tea.

"If you wanted to save up some cash," she explains.

"When is Mercy getting out?" The question pops out of my mouth. I want to take it back, to pretend I don't care.

She eyes me knowingly. "May." Clasping her hands in her lap, she purses her lips.

"May," I repeat. That's in five months. I lean back into the couch. If only I'd asked yesterday, I wouldn't have been such a mess today.

"What is it with you two?" she muses. "You're all he ever asks about—and Olivia, of course."

I want to strangle her for even saying my daughter's name.

"Twenty years, and he still only has eyes for you." Her eyes drop down to her lap, her fingers twisting. "He made a mistake," she murmurs. "*I* made a mistake."

I stand. "What's for dinner?" Turning from her, I carry my empty mug to the sink.

"You mean you didn't cook?"

I peer at her over my shoulder.

She grins at me from across the room. "I'm teasing. I know you don't cook." Standing, she stretches. "I figured I'd make some chicken soup. Sound good?"

A homewrecker who can cook. Claudine is full of surprises. In another life, I might even like her. I shrug, then slip past her to the front door. "I'm going for a walk."

"See you for dinner," she says.

* * *

The next week passes with us repeating the same steps every day. Claudine goes to work while I occupy myself around the house. She jokes that it's cleaner than it's ever been with me around. Every afternoon when she gets home, she asks if I'm staying for dinner.

"For tonight," I reply.

While we clean up the kitchen, she reminds me about the porter job, and I remind her that I'm just a waitress with a gaping resume.

"I've been with the hospital for ten years," she always says. "I can get you in on my good word alone."

We don't talk about Mercy.

I lie awake at night, knowing I need to make a decision. Pick a direction. Just begin—again. The truth is, I'm tired of running. Seeing the home that Claudine made for herself makes me wonder if I could have a home too, had I tried.

Then I remember that I *did* try, and she ruined it all.

On a Friday night almost two weeks after I arrived, Claudine comes home looking paper thin. I stir the canned tomato soup on the stove, check the sandwiches on the griddle. She slumps into a seat at the kitchen table.

Whatever is wrong, it's none of my business. Or so I tell myself. I put down a bowl of soup and a plate of grilled cheese in front of her, then take the seat across from her with my own food. "Rough day?"

I can't help it. I've always enjoyed talking to people. It's what makes me such a good waitress.

"One of my patients died." She pushes her spoon around the bowl but doesn't take a bite.

"Oh." I set down my grilled cheese. I don't know what to say.

"She was young," Claudine continues, as if I'd asked. "Around Olivia's age. She'd been drinking. Hit a guard rail and flipped over it. There wasn't much we could do."

I squeeze my eyes shut.

"Don't you ever think about her?" she asks in a whisper.

"Don't," I warn.

I did the right thing.

"Why not? Bree, how could you walk away from your little girl?"

My eyes fly open. "How could you sleep with my husband?"

We glare at each other across the table.

"Mercy gets out in four months," she says. "Don't you think it's time you face your family?"

"What makes you think you even have a right to ask me that?"

"Because I owe you, damn it," she says, eyes shining. "People grow up, Bree. I've counted my mistakes, and I'm just trying to atone for them."

"By hanging out with the other woman? By grilling me for answers you don't have the right to?" My nostrils flare.

"You're right. I don't deserve answers from you. But Mercy and Olivia do."

I stare at her.

"Your daughter is graduating college this spring," she says, flinging the words at me.

My jaw falls open.

"She's going to be a social worker." She stirs her soup as if she's still going to eat it. "Don't you want to make things right?"

"I did the right thing," I insist. "She deserved better. There was nothing left between Mercy and me."

"Wasn't there?" She keeps stirring, a slow circle.

"We weren't supposed to be together, anyway. Then he went away. What was I supposed to do, Claudine?" Tears sting my eyes. "I had this little baby to take care of, and I was still a baby, myself."

"You had help," she says, reaching across the table for my hand. Her eyes are too kind.

"Help." I scoff, hugging myself. "Everything was falling apart."

"Bree," she pleads, "you have to talk to someone. Shannon tried to help you. God knows Mercy tried."

"Mercy chose the club over me—over our family." My hands clench into fists.

She smiles. "Now we're getting somewhere."

"What are you, my therapist?" I stand from the table, pacing the tiny kitchen.

"I'm just the cunt who slept with your husband, who's trying to make things right," she says with a shrug. "It's not like I can ever get back into Ravage's good graces. What do you have to lose here?"

"I've already lost it all," I tell her.

"Then get it back. Fight, Bree. *Fight*."

I shake my head at her. I don't know how. All I know is how to run.

PART II

THE WAR HERO

8

1997

I might have lost my mind.

Not that the war didn't already do that for me.

But I asked the club's newest cocktail waitress to be my fake ol' lady, and then I went and made plans with Shannon behind my President's back. My best friend's back.

Not that I really knew who he was, not anymore.

I'd never been able to say no to Shannon. I was only a year older than her, but she still had that baby sister voodoo on me. Bree was her latest project. I should've stayed the hell away—I had my own project to worry about. I probably would've stayed out of it, but then Bastard had to go and slap my sister.

Shannon didn't need to worry about Ravage, because *I* was going to fucking kill Bastard myself.

I put a lid on my anger for the time being. All in due time. I'd never been one to blow up; I've always been more of a thinker. I could plot my way through a dozen kinds of revenge. I moved up quickly through the Army because I never lost my cool in combat, and my superiors respected that. It also got me a nice case of PTSD, but what can you do?

Bree eyed me warily from across the bar. There were wars waging in her eyes.

"He'll behave," Shannon encouraged her. "He'd have to answer to me."

I pulled my lips back in an exaggerated grimace.

Bree smiled. Even though it shouldn't have mattered to me, it sent a rush of warmth through my limbs, warmer than any booze on the planet. She took a deep breath, her dark eyes fixed on mine. "Okay," she said.

"Good." Shannon shooed her out from behind the bar. "I just heard Bastard take off on his bike. You go get your things together, and I'll be up in a moment to show you Mercy's room."

Tossing me a tentative smile, Bree did as she was told.

She always did.

I watched her go, my own smile fading. I turned to my sister. "I don't know about this, Shan."

Her eyes flashed. "I need you on board, Mercer. Someone hurt that sweet thing, and someone's got to take care of her."

"So your solution is to marry her off to a biker?"

"Well, you don't have to get married . . ." She grinned. "Just be good to her."

"I'm not dating her," I warned.

"I know."

"I've got my own shit to work through."

"I know," she said again.

"Okay." I picked up my shot glass and held it out to her.

"So what are you gonna say to Bastard?" she asked, pouring me a fresh shot.

"I don't know, Shan." I downed it, keeping the glass in my hand. I turned it around and around, watching the glass catch the light. "That goddamn war screwed us all up, but I'm starting to think he wasn't all right in the first place."

"What do you mean?"

"I mean," I said, still twisting the glass, "he's always got this air of someone who's just done something wrong and doesn't give a fuck if he gets caught. I don't know how to explain it."

"You mean his little side business?" she asked, polishing a glass, a wry smile on her lips.

"It was my idea. We voted that in. I know Ravage told you that."

She lifted a shoulder. "You better watch out before this club becomes a cliche. I told Ravage *that*."

"It isn't nothing that anyone else in this town isn't already doing. We're just saving the vets who hang around with us from having to skulk around the back parking lot while they wait for their dealer."

Shaking her head at me, she turned, almost dancing as she moved here and there, putting away glasses. "I also told Ravage there's no way in hell our girls are muling."

I sighed. "That's for the club to decide, Shannon."

"It's not happening."

I was starting to see why Bastard lost his temper on her. He shouldn't have hit her, but the club was none of her business. She meant well, though. "I'll tell you what," I said, standing. "Ravage and I will both vote nay on the girls, if it comes to the table."

She beamed at me as she put one last glass away. "I'll go get your bride settled in."

"Ha," I said dryly. "This is only 'til you find her something more permanent."

"Who knows?" she said, eyes gleaming. "Maybe I won't have to."

* * *

I cruised down 63 toward Bastard's apartment. *Sebastian*, I reminded myself. *His name is Sebastian.*

Second Lieutenants Demmel and Reynolds—those were our names then, in that dusty hell. I shuddered, the bike vibrating underneath me. We'd enlisted in the Reserve, which paid for both of our college degrees. We'd both done the ROTC program, which skyrocketed us to O-1 rank. Neither of us ever thought we'd be deployed. We wanted to open a business together. I'd majored in business management and he majored in marketing; together, we were going to open a strip club and start a motorcycle club with our friends.

It was a simple dream. We both longed for freedom and brotherhood, a bonded home that would replace our conservative, judgmental families. Sebastian met Ruth in high school and they had Cliff when they were still babies themselves. His family disowned him, so he took Ruth and went to a YMCA. It seemed like a good time to follow him.

Most teen parents end up dropping out, but not Bastard—not even Ruth. They were both determined. The three of us kept each other motivated, doling out tough love as needed. I'd always liked Ruth, but she became like a sister to me. And when Cliff was born, both of them agreed I'd be his godfather.

I'd never been anything to anyone, but when I held that tiny baby, I promised him I'd do whatever it took to keep him safe, to teach him about the world, and to support his dreams.

Part of that promise meant keeping Sebastian in check.

He'd always tasted just a little bitter. Most people stayed away from him. After the war—the whole four days it lasted—he got worse, but even before that, there was something just off about him. There was this need to control. At first, I chalked it up to his Type A, business-minded free bird strain. I'd loved him since we were awkward teenage boys battling acne and failing at guitar. But sometimes, he needed to hurt people, and I couldn't justify that.

I just didn't know what to do about it.

Sebastian had given me a home, a real place to belong. He'd accepted me without question, taking me in as his friend during a time when I was vulnerable and confused, my body speeding through changes. He'd been by my side through college, in the Kuwait theater while bombs rained around us and strangers shot at us, and through everything after the war. He was the only person who knew what I was going through, because he was living it, too.

I owed him more than I could ever give, starting with being there for him through whatever he was dealing with.

Even if I wanted to strangle him for hitting my sister.

I slowed to a stop in front of the house he rented. He was the only member of the club who didn't sleep in the club house. Both of us received enough VA comp to buy nice houses, but I didn't want to be alone and he didn't want to deal with the upkeep.

Or so he told the guys.

I knew the truth: Ruth didn't want Cliff having anything to do with the club. And, by extension, that included me. Even with her gone a decade, I respected her wishes. For the most part.

Cliff, Bastard's seventeen-year-old, sat on the front steps, headphones on, music almost loud enough to hear over the Softail. I cut the engine, holding a hand up in greeting. He nodded back, tipping his head down.

I frowned.

"What's up?" I strolled over, noting the cigarette in his hand. I could harp on him for that later. I'd smoked my share of cancer sticks over in theater, and quit the day I touched American soil again. Bastard, on the other hand, was cultivating lung cancer, and apparently so was his kid.

Cliff shrugged.

"You all right?" I leaned on the porch railing, giving him space but standing close enough that we could talk.

He shrugged again, his brown eyes dark.

Teenage angst, or Bastard?

A car pulled up behind my bike. Ignoring it, I focused on my godson. His eyes tracked the car, lighting up. Doors closed and a tiny voice rang out. "Cliffy!" Grinning, Cliff stood, pulling off his headphones in time to catch the little girl who flew into his arms.

"Hey, Luce."

"Wanna play Crash?"

"Of course." A look of fierce adoration held fast in his eyes. He set her down, gently taking her hand.

I knew exactly how he felt about his little cousin Lucy. I'd do anything for him, my godson. I'd die for him, because I loved him as much as I loved his parents. Maybe even more.

They disappeared inside, the little girl chatting while Cliff listened patiently. I stood on the porch a moment longer, watching the car pull away from the curb. I scoffed. Sebastian's family hated him, but when they needed a babysitter so they could go out and party, they had no problem using him.

It was just as well. Lucy seemed happiest with Cliff, and she had the same effect on him. I hoped someday I'd have kids of my own that he'd be close with. It was a silly thought—I was lightyears away from so much as looking at a woman, never mind settling down. Still, it comforted me.

Someday, I could have a real family.

I walked into the house, passing the living room where Cliff was setting up the PlayStation. I found Sebastian in the dormant garden out back.

"Hey," I said, bending down next to him. I grabbed a handful of dead weeds and yanked them out of the earth. "Lucy just got here."

He grunted as he tugged at a stubborn rock.

Shannon was wrong when she said I needed to approach him carefully. I'd never beat around the bush with my best friend before, and I wasn't about to start. "So," I said, closing my fingers around another rock. "What's going on?"

His jaw tightened. "What do you mean?"

"You can't go around slapping people you disagree with," I said. "Especially not one of our own people. What's up with you? Is it the PTSD?"

He scoffed. "Here we go."

"You're damn right." I tossed the rock to the side. "I love you, man, but I'm not gonna pretend you didn't hit my sister. I'm about two seconds away from clocking you. What the fuck?"

His pale blue eyes flashed.

Wiping my hands on my jeans, I stood, grimacing at the ache in my knees and hips. "Nothing? You know you can play the PTSD card and I'll get it. Just talk to me, Sebastian."

"Bastard," he corrected, standing and lighting a cigarette.

"All right, tough guy." I sighed. "You know you can talk to me. Normally I'd say take your time, but I'm surprised Ravage isn't already breaking down your door. Look, I don't know what's going on with you lately, but you've got to get your shit handled."

He smirked. "Yeah? How's that working out for you?" He nodded toward me. "You handling *your* shit?"

"Totally different, man. I'm not slapping people to work through my pain."

"Just smoking weed and selling it."

I held up my hands. "You sound like Shannon. It helps a lot of people. I thought you were on board with this."

"I am."

"So you're just lashing out at me," I said, nodding. "Sounds like PTSD to me."

"Think whatever you want." He sucked down his cigarette, then tossed it into the cold dirt.

"What's going on with Cliff?" I asked.

He lit another cigarette. "Who knows."

"For fuck's sake, *Bastard*. He's your kid."

"You're right," he snapped. "My kid. My club."

"So it's like that now, huh? I thought this was our baby." I tried to shake off his words. He was just being defensive.

Using his thumb, he poked at his PRESIDENT patch.

"Yeah, all right." Sighing, I turned back toward the house.

"Rules are rules for a reason," he said.

I paused, waiting for him to say more. At least we were finally getting to the meat of it. His problem wasn't with Shannon or me. It was Bree.

"She's not a member."

"She's not," I agreed, "but she is my . . . ol' lady. We were trying to take things slow."

"I don't like her," he snapped.

I frowned. "Bree? Why not?" As far as I could tell, Bree had gone out of her way to stay out of the club's way. She did everything everyone asked her, picking up extra shifts when there were gaps. Shannon adored her.

But Bastard wouldn't elaborate, and I knew better than to poke the bear. "Will you at least apologize to Shannon? We don't need the table getting any more split."

"I ain't apologizing. She needs to know her place."

Maybe I needed to take the bear out with a tranquilizer.

I rubbed my hands together, warming my stiff joints. I'd left my gloves with the bike. It figured. I couldn't fix anything—not my mystery illness, not my godson, not my best friend. At least I'd made Bree happy. In turn, I'd helped Shannon. It didn't make up for Bastard hitting her, but it was a start.

"You know Ravage is gonna take this to the table," I said. "How are you going to handle that?"

He shrugged.

"I'm gonna have to back him up. She's my sister, Bastard. And we don't hit women."

He shrugged again.

I gaped at him. "Really? Nothing?"

"You want my throne," he said, eyes empty, "come and get it."

I left him in the frozen garden, mind reeling. Something had happened to my best friend, and it was going to destroy us all if I wasn't careful.

9

NOW

I leave my godson in a cloud of dust, almost regretting it. Mostly because he doesn't seem to remember me, but it's been twenty years. Cliff was a kid last time I saw him. Memory is a fickle creature.

I can't sit and chat with him, though, because if I do, I'll never leave. There are a million reasons why I should stay, all of them beginning and ending with Olivia. My little girl. I miss her so much, my chest aches. I've made many mistakes, but she's the best thing I did. And if I'm going to make things right, I've got to start with her mother.

Bree.

The difference between Olivia and Bree is, my daughter is a fighter. She plants her feet and doesn't budge until whatever it is, is settled. I know this because Ravage and Shannon told me everything about her while I was inside. Even the small details, like what she ate during a morning shift at The Wet Mermaid.

My wife, however, is a runner. The moment she set foot in The Wet Mermaid, Shannon knew she was running from something. She hasn't stopped since.

I should've chased her.

I can't turn back time. All I can do is move forward, and now that I'm out, I'm doing what I should've done a long time ago.

I'm chasing her.

I ease up on the throttle, my knuckles aching. Every joint in my body has ached since I was twenty-seven—when I landed in the Kuwait theater. I'll never forget the moment it all started, the zing that radiated from my wrist to my elbow, a sensation I'd never felt before. At the time, I had no idea what was happening to me. None of us knew.

I shouldn't be riding down to Virginia, not in my condition. The twenty years I spent in Lewisburg were not kind to me. I should've hopped onto a train from Lewisburg, but I couldn't stand the thought of leaving my Softail in that garage another minute.

My plan is simple: ride for as long as I can, then stop at a motel, preferably one with a working ice machine so I can take an ice bath and then a hot shower. Officially, the VA calls it Chronic Multisymptom Illness. But we refer to it as Gulf War Syndrome.

There's no treatment. I'm lucky the VA even acknowledges it as this point. At least I got a nice house out of it. A house that, once upon a time, I hoped my family would grow in.

That was all shattered though, in an instant. And then I had to go and put the pieces six feet under.

Like I said, I've made my share of mistakes.

I've lived. I've learned. And now I'm fighting like hell to make things right.

As right as I can.

I just hope that when I get to Virginia, she'll stick around long enough to hear me out. Hell, I hope she hasn't already started running.

Goddamn Claudine. She should've kept her mouth shut. That's Claudine, though. She can't keep a secret, not even if her life depends on it. No matter how well her intentions are.

I haven't spoken to her in a couple of weeks, so all I can do is hope that, for once, Bree's and my timelines line up.

10

1997

For the most part, I stayed away from the room Bree and I shared. I spent more and more time outside of The Wet Mermaid, away from the club. The club and my life hung upside down, and I dangled from its cracking ceiling.

Late on a Saturday night, I trudged up the stairs, away from the blare of the music downstairs. My knees ached with every step. It was one of those days where nothing was working, and I'd taken more Advil than my liver probably cared to handle. Sighing, I reached the door to my room. Light shone from underneath. I hadn't seen Bree downstairs, so she must've had a rare night off.

Lifting a fist pocked with swollen knuckles, I hesitated. Knocking on my own door. I should just walk in. It was my room, too, after all. Still, for all I knew, she'd just taken a shower or something. The club house rooms were like studio apartments or motel rooms: a single room with a coffee maker and microwave, and a private bathroom. Miles above the barracks I'd lived in, but not exactly homey.

I tapped my knuckles against the wood, wincing as hot pain radiated through my hand.

"Who is it?" she called out in her sweet voice.

"It's me." I ran a hand through my hair. "Can I come in?"

The door opened. She faced me with an amused smile. "It's your room." She stepped aside.

"Yours too," I replied as I moved out of the hall. I glanced around, taking in the little touches she'd added. Indigo curtains, with an actual bed set that matched. Candles on the nightstand, framed art on the walls and dresser. I stood in front of a large canvas filled with a human face, the mouth open in a scream, eyes pinched in anguish, the hands cradling the cheeks. The artist used muted blues, oranges, and grays. I stared, transfixed.

It was exactly how I felt.

"I probably should've asked before doing all this," she apologized from beside me.

"No," I said, turning. "It looks good." I gave her what I hoped was a reassuring smile. "Besides—"

"It's my room, too." She grinned, her smile lighting up the room. "So you like it?"

"Yeah." I lifted a hand. "Where did you get all this?"

"Oh, here and there. Mostly tag sales. There's a woman who walks up and down 63, pushing all her paintings in a cart. She makes jewelry, too." She sighed wistfully. "She's got this beautiful turquoise ring that I will never be able to afford."

"Is her name Phee, by chance?"

Her eyes lit up. "You know her?"

"I've known her since she was Charlie. She was in my unit in the theater—in Kuwait." I studied the painting again. It made perfect sense. Phee knew exactly how I felt because she lived with it, too. The only difference was, she numbed her mysterious pain with booze and acid.

"You're a veteran," Bree said.

I nodded, stepping away from the painting. I went to the dresser and opened the top drawer. "Do you mind?" I asked, holding up a joint.

"Not at all." She sat down on the bed, watching me.

"Do you smoke?" I pulled a Zippo out of my pocket and lit the joint.

"Sometimes." The corner of her mouth twisted up, her eyes dancing.

I brought the joint to my lips, taking a long hit while I tried not to stare. Her eyes pulled me in, so bright, a hazel joyful brown usually tinged with wariness. Not when she looked at me, though. When she looked at me, she let her joy shine.

Shannon was right. Someone had hurt her—bad.

I didn't know why she was less guarded around me. Maybe because of Shannon. My sister always had a way of soothing people, making them feel safe. Maybe Bree felt safe around me by association.

I held the joint out to her. She took it, her fingers careful not to touch mine or the burning end. "Recreational?" she asked, little puffs of smoking escaping her lips. "Or . . . ?"

"Or," I replied, flexing my hands.

"Does it help?"

"For the most part. The cold makes it worse, though." I pulled out the lone chair I kept in the room and sat down.

"Arthritis?" She tilted her head, taking another hit. "No," she exhaled. "You're too young."

I laughed. "I'm older than you, Eighteen."

"So it is arthritis." She passed the joint back to me.

"Sort of." I held the smoke in my mouth, trying to ignore the acrid taste. My limbs tingled with a pleasant dullness. Beneath that, though, I still felt the hot knives searing my joints. I sighed.

We smoked in silence for several minutes, handing the joint back and forth until it threatened to burn fingers. I died out the roach in an ashtray, then leaned back in my seat.

She sprawled on the bed like a cat, gazing at the ceiling. "Ever wish this feeling could last forever?"

"All the time." My body sank heavily in the chair, yet floated.

It was a different warmth, one that chased away the inflammation. I wanted to ask her what pain she was trying to dull.

"War injury?" she asked, beating me to it.

My eyes flicked to Phee's painting while I debated how to answer. I wasn't sure, myself. "War side effect, I guess."

"What do your doctors say?"

I laughed, the sound bitter. "They say it's all in my head. There's nothing physically wrong with me."

"But you're in pain." She sat up, folding her legs.

"Yes."

"All the time."

I nodded.

"And they don't have any answers for you?"

"We vets call it Gulf War Syndrome. Most of us have it. Mine started when I was still over there."

"Then it can't be in your head."

I shrugged. "For the longest time, it didn't exist—according to the VA."

"And nothing really helps? Other than smoking yourself sober?"

"Mild weather," I said. "Ice baths."

She grimaced. "Sounds brutal."

"They are. But they help, in a way."

"I guess, if you're trying to numb yourself up."

"Or cool the burn."

We grinned at each other.

"Well," she said, turning back the comforter. "I've got to go to sleep. I'm not a pro like you."

I stood. "Goodnight, Bree."

"Goodnight, Mercy."

I edged out of the room and headed downstairs where my Softail waited. For a while I rode around town, enjoying the cold wind in my hair until I could no longer keep my eyes open. I returned to my room and made myself comfortable on the floor.

Still better than the barracks.

I woke early in the afternoon, the sun almost at the top of the sky, Bree long gone. On the nightstand sat a metal pot labeled with a magic marker: Mercy Balm. I twisted off the lid and sniffed it. The spicy scent of camphor made my eyes water. Underneath it, I detected clove and menthol. I dipped a finger in the salve and patted some on my knuckles. Almost right away, the zinging pain in my joints faded.

I held the little pot in my hand, closed my fingers around it, and brought it to my chest.

11

NOW

It'll take several days and several motels before I cross the Virginia state line. One of the pluses of being a River Reaper is a percentage of all club business, even while I was inside. I've got to remember to sit Cliff down when I get back and set him up with Bastard's inheritance. It's not a whole lot, but it'll help some.

I'm still several days from Claudine's condo. A younger me could push on through, get there sometime early in the morning, when it's still dark enough and late enough that it's really just night. The Mercy before the war didn't need to take breaks every hour. But the Mercy after the war needs a hot meal and a good smoke. These bones need to rest.

I veer into the motel parking lot, the headlight streaking across the side of the building. I back the bike into a spot real slow, my hips and wrists stiff and screaming. I pushed it a little too far this last stretch.

Soon I won't be able to ride at all anymore.

Not after four months in the theater and twenty years in prison.

This body is no longer mine.

I use my hands to pull my leg over the side of the bike, wincing as something in my joints cracks. The beginning of the end.

Chasing Bree might kill me.

Limping, I make my way to the office. Just like all motels, the lighting is dim and yellow, both jarring and subduing all at once.

"Welcome to Singh Inn," the bored looking young woman behind the desk says. She fusses with long, inky hair, brown eyes giving me an up and down sweep. She blinks twice. "Sir!" she exclaims. "Can I help you?"

I must look pretty bad.

Waving her off, I lean on the counter. "I just need a room for the night."

"Double or king?" she asks, brow furrowed.

"Whatever you've got." I pull my wallet from my back pocket.

"A king, then," she says, tapping away at the computer.

I glance around the lobby. "Did you say Singh Inn?"

She nods, her eyes remaining on the screen.

"Swear I stayed in another Singh Inn last night," I mutter.

"Oh yes," she says, taking the credit card I hand her. "We're all over the East Coast, from Connecticut down to Virginia. We pretty much dot Route 13. Family owned and operated." She slides the card back to me. "You can use Uber Eats if you're hungry."

I blink at her. I don't even know exactly where I am, never mind what an uber might eat.

"The app? They deliver here all the time." Her musical accent rocks me back and forth. She activates my room key and passes it over.

"Thanks," I tell her.

Outside, I grab my bag then go find my room. I'm running through the standard options, trying to figure out whether I'm in the mood for pizza or Chinese, when it hits me. I've been ordering food from motel rooms. I can just call Claudine. I've memorized her number after all the years making calls from inside.

I swipe the key through the reader, then push into the room. It's exactly the same as every motel room I've ever been in. There must be some sort of owners' manual they pass out when you open one. Dropping my bag by the door, I go straight to the phone.

My ankle gives out halfway across the room.

I stumble, nearly falling flat on my face. I right myself at the last second and hobble back over to the door. Even after all these years, I'm still not used to the sensation. One of the doctors I saw inside—the only one to ever even try to help me—said my symptoms reminded him of a cross between tendonitis and Fibromyalgia. He gave me some Tylenol and one of those emergency ice packs.

That was the extent of my Lewisburg medical care.

Grabbing the saddlebag, I limp to the bed. I use my good ankle—good for the moment, anyway—and sit down, scooting back onto the mattress. Then I dump the saddlebag onto the bedspread.

I didn't pack much—I didn't need much. Just some cash, the credit card Beer Can said was still good last time we talked, a few T-shirts, clean underwear. And the things that Beer Can packed for me.

I hold the dropper bottle of CBD oil in my hand, marveling at how far medicine has come since the nineties. According to the note Beer Can left me, a few drops of this every day should decrease the inflammation in my body over time.

I pick up the long, thin cigarette shaped vape pen. Beer Can said a few hits of this will help control the pain. So far, I don't feel like the CBD oil is making much of a difference. Maybe I need to be patient. But the vaporized THC helps.

I drip a few drops of the oil onto my tongue and swallow, then take a few hits off the pen. Within moments I feel less pain. I'll have to grab some ice in a minute and put my ankle up for a while.

But first, Bree.

I scoot backward on the bed 'til I can reach the phone. They'll probably charge the long distance call to my credit card—I'm somewhere in Maryland—but it's worth it. I punch in the area code and then Claudine's number, pulse thrumming. I can already hear Bree's voice.

What will we say to each other after all these years? Are there even any words?

The phone rings.

12

1997

I jogged down the club house stairs, lighter than I'd been in years. Bree's balm not only soothed my joints, but also my soul. I couldn't remember the last time anyone cared enough to do something like that for me.

Her balm wasn't a cure, but it reinvigorated me. I couldn't wait to thank her.

As I hit the landing, I almost crashed into Ravage. He grabbed my elbow and steered me toward a dark corner of the bar.

"I was just coming up for you," he said, lips barely moving. He dropped into a seat and picked up his whiskey.

I took the seat opposite him. "I talked to him," I began, picking my words carefully. Ravage loved my sister as much as I did. Bastard might as well be riding on black ice.

But he shook his head, icy blue eyes flashing. "This isn't about Shannon." His eyes focused on something behind me, then swept the room. His gaze returned to me. "This is . . ." He slugged down the rest of the whiskey. "I'm in over my head here, Mercer."

I snapped to attention. I couldn't remember him ever using my actual name. "What's going on?"

His lips pursed, eyes drifting to Bree. She sauntered over in her heels, her smile friendly and zeroed in on me.

"Refill?" she asked, nodding to Ravage's empty glass.

"Please." He flashed her a relaxed smile, a complete about face from the heavy way his skin hung on his skull two seconds earlier.

I frowned, mind reeling as I tried imagining what could be worse than Bastard slapping Shannon. The threat he'd laid out echoed through my thoughts: *Come and take it from me.* Surely Ravage wasn't talking about *that*. Bastard was going through something, but I was confident that he'd level out. The club was in no danger.

We'd worked too hard to build it.

I'd worked too hard.

"And for you?" Bree asked.

"I'll have the same."

She nodded.

Before she walked away, I caught her hand. The chair underneath me might as well have been anchored to the ceiling, but Bree grounded me. "Thanks for the balm," I told her.

She squeezed my hand, her touch gentle. "Any time." Flashing me another smile, she strutted away.

I gazed after her, my chest warm.

"Mercer," Ravage snapped, drawing me back to the moment.

I dragged my eyes from Bree's retreating form and made myself look at my brother. My friend. "What's all this about?"

He leaned across the table. "We have to vote taking Bastard to the river."

I stared at him. "Todd." His first name fell from my lips, a plea. "What the fuck are you talking about?"

"I'm coming to you first as VP, but I'm taking this to the table no matter what comes out of this discussion. Do you understand?"

Even as I swayed from the ceiling, I marveled at how someday, he'd make a great President. Better than Bastard. Certainly better than I could.

Bree set our drinks down and hurried away, the club filling up around us. She tossed me a wink over her shoulder. I barely noticed.

I took a swig of the whiskey. "Tell me what you're talking about."

"I was pissed about Shannon," he said. "I took a ride out to his house the other night to talk to him." He swept the club again.

I'd never seen him so on edge.

"I've got a key from the last time I house sat for them, so I let myself in." His eyes darkened. "I had every intention of beating the shit out of him."

I nodded. I knew the feeling.

"The house was dark, but I heard . . . crying. A little girl." He swirled the whiskey in his glass, eyes boring into the liquid as if he could set it on fire. "She was begging him to stop."

His niece Lucy. My stomach cramped, bile rising in my throat.

He slugged back the rest of his whiskey, slamming down the glass. "Mercy, I swear to fucking God, I was gonna rip his head off."

"So why didn't you?" I spat. I shoved my chair back.

"Wait," he commanded, glancing around again. "We take this to the table." He struck the tip of his index finger against the table, tapping it with force.

I put my head in my hands. "Why are you telling me this? How can I sit with this and not kill him myself?"

He wrenched my wrists from my face. "Because we're a club, and we have a code to follow. Do you really think anyone at that table is going to vote no?"

I shook my head again as my brain finally caught up. Bastard had to go. He'd crossed line after line, and enough was enough. But by bringing this to the table with Ravage, I'd be sentencing my best friend to death. Maybe even by my own hand.

There was no choice. My vote was yea. I didn't even have to think about it. There would be consequences, repercussions that we'd have to deal with.

"Cliff," I said to Ravage.

He nodded. "We'll take care of him. Watch out for him. When he's eighteen, we'll make him a Prospect."

I rubbed my face with my hands. I needed a drink, but my stomach roiled at the thought of more whiskey. "Ruth is rolling in her grave," I said. I sat up straight, jaw falling.

"What?"

I thought of the protective way Cliff watched Lucy, the hunch of his shoulders, the set of his jaw. He knew. Or, if he didn't know, he suspected. "Where was Cliff when you went into the house?"

"No one saw me, if that's what you're getting at." Ravage lit a cigarette, his stomach apparently calm enough.

I wished things had been different, that Ruth had allowed Cliff around the club. I could've been the godfather I should've been. When she died, I thought for sure I could at least be there for him, but her aunt swooped in and kept the boy close. She'd filled Ruth's shoes over the years, but she'd been old even back then. She passed away not long before Bree turned up. As it stood, Cliff wouldn't have anybody once we took care of Bastard. He barely knew any of us. I doubted he'd want anything to do with the club. God only knew what he thought of us, especially if he suspected Bastard was hurting Lucy.

If we couldn't convince him to be a Prospect, we'd be making him an orphan. He was weeks away from eighteen, but still. He was only a kid.

I dragged my hands through my hair.

"This is fucked up," Ravage said, as if reading my thoughts.

"When do you want to take the vote?"

"Soon." His lips pursed.

I looked up. Bastard swung toward our table, his face twisted in a grin I couldn't read. I didn't know him at all anymore. He was a monster, always had been underneath. He'd just shed the remaining layer of his human skin.

Standing, I gave him a nod, forcing myself to meet his eyes. Until we took the vote, I had to pretend everything was normal. If he caught on, it'd all be over.

13

NOW

I swear, the motel room actually dims while I wait for someone to pick up. Or maybe it's because I'm holding my breath. I let it out and the phone rings and rings.

"Damn it, Claudine," I mutter.

Halfway through a particularly long ring, it stops. There's a click and a shuffle, and then the clearing of a throat.

"Hello?" Bree demands more than says.

My heart stops.

The entire muscle seizes in my chest. The familiar warmth that always fills me when she's around floods my ribcage, stealing my breath away again.

"Hello?" She's even more annoyed now.

"Bree." Her name falls from my lips like a prayer. She's still there. I didn't miss her. She didn't run.

Silence.

"Bree?" If it weren't for the static, I'd think we got disconnected. Got to love Claudine and her stubborn clinging to the landline. As far as I know, she still doesn't even have caller ID. Just an old rotary phone in the kitchen. She once told me it was because it's so satisfying to slam the phone onto the receiver.

"You're out," Bree says.

"I'm out," I confirm.

The static buzzes between us, shifting to a higher pitched hum.

"Have you seen Olivia?"

I love that the first thing she asks me is about our daughter. Bree always thought she'd be an awful mom, but a bad mother wouldn't even care enough to ask. A bad mother wouldn't care enough to consider whether she'd be a good mother. A bad mother wouldn't have made the choice to give Olivia a better life.

"Not yet," I confess.

"Oh." Her voice is so small.

I picture her standing in the kitchen, twisting the cord around her fingers. The image is so vivid, I almost believe it's real, that I can just reach out and still her hands. "She's doing okay," I promise.

"How do you know, when you haven't even seen her?" She sighs. "I thought I could count on you for at least that."

I lick my lips. Typical Bree, lashing out at me when she feels dizzy inside. I don't take it personally. Never have. Those sharp words aren't my Bree—they're the PTSD talking, her brain's defense mechanism.

I would know.

"Ravage updated me every week," I soothe.

"Well, all right, if *Todd* kept you informed."

"He's her godfather, Bree. He's taken good care of her for us."

She says nothing.

"I didn't stop in to see Olivia because if I did, I never would've left."

I hear her inhale through her nose, but she remains wordless.

"I haven't seen her in person since she was a baby," I say, the words catching in my throat. My eyes burn, my arms remembering the soft weight of Olivia in my arms.

"That was your choice," she reminds me.

"I know," I say. "I'm not throwing it in your face, Bree. I'd do it all again. I'm just saying—"

"Would you 'do it all again'?" she demands. "Knowing how this all turned out?"

"Yes," I say without hesitating. "Bree . . ." I sigh. I don't know what I thought would happen. I've never had the magic words to convince her. I've only ever had my actions, keeping my promises even when it punishes me, and even those have never convinced her.

She keeps running, and I don't know how to slow her down long enough.

"Are you coming to Claudine's?" she asks.

"I am."

"Why?" she whispers, the one tiny word brimming with pain.

I suck in a deep breath. "Because you're my wife."

She scoffs. "Don't you think I've punished you enough?"

"You've never punished me," I remind her. "Remember, this was all my idea. I've only done it to myself." I keep my tone light, even thought what we're talking about is anything but.

"Why?" she asks again.

Because it was the right thing. Because she always did nice things for me. Because in this incredibly fucked up world, she is the only thing that has ever made sense to me—her and Olivia.

I don't say these things because I know they'll only send her running again. "Just come home with me," I say instead. "Then we can both see our daughter."

She sighs again, a pained tearless cry. "I can't," she whispers.

"You can. We'll do it together."

"How can I even begin to explain to her?" she asks, her voice crushed feathers.

"I don't know," I say, because this isn't the time for placating lies. "But we'll do it together."

"You keep saying that."

"Yes." I chuckle. "I'm your husband, Bree. We both said the words: for better, for worse."

"What if I don't want to be married anymore?"

"Did you ever want to be married?" I joke.

"What if I met someone else?"

I freeze. "Someone else?" I stutter. I hadn't even considered it. Not in the entire twenty years we've been apart.

"What if?" she presses.

My blood starts moving in my veins again. "Hypotheticals don't matter."

"Don't they? It's been twenty years, Mercy."

I start at the sound of my name. It's the first time I've heard her say it tonight.

"It's all done and over with now," she continues. "You can move on with your life—meet someone else."

"What if I don't want to meet anyone else?"

"Hypotheticals don't matter," she says, and hangs up.

I close my eyes in defeat. I was so close. There's no point in even going to Claudine's now, because I know Bree is already packing. I don't know where she'll go next, but I'll still follow her.

If running is all Bree knows, then chasing her is all I know.

14

1997

I trudged up the stairs to the club house rooms, my thoughts smashing into each other, stomach churning. I'd known Bastard for practically a lifetime, but in an instant I found out I didn't really know him at all. All I wanted was a shower hot enough to melt my skin, slough away the acidic truth eating at me. Then a long, long ride around town—maybe even out of the state.

I pushed open the door to my room and stumbled in, limbs shocked rather than drunk.

"Well this is awkward," Bree said.

I jumped, pulse kicking up another thousand notches. There might as well be bullets and bombs raining on me.

"You all right?" she asked.

I faced her. She sat crosslegged on the bed, one of my black T-shirts covering her like a long nightgown.

"Shannon ran my things over to the laundromat," she explained quickly. "I swear I'll give it back. I thought you were out for the day."

"What are you, a spill magnet?" I shook my head at her, amused.

"Always and forever." Her smile fell. "What's wrong?"

"Is it that obvious?" I muttered. I couldn't feign levity around her, not when she was the only person who truly saw me. I slumped into the chair.

"Some people used to tell me I'm a good listener."

"Used to?" I lifted an eyebrow at her, grateful for the change of subject. "Where are your people, Bree?"

"They aren't my people anymore." She tugged the hem of the shirt farther down her thighs, even though my 3XLT shirt almost fell to her calves, she was so tiny. "What happened?"

I sighed, wishing there was someone I could talk to. That someone couldn't be Bree. It was clear she had enough of her own problems.

"I'm your ol' lady," she prodded. "You can tell me anything."

"Thought you were my fake ol' lady," I said, a smile tugging at my lips.

"So fake tell me anything." She folded her hands and lifted her chin attentively. "I'm all fake ears. Besides, I could use the distraction."

"All right." I stood and went to the dresser, pulling out my kit. "This is a smoking conversation, though."

"Then I should probably pass."

I glanced at her over my shoulder. "Why?"

"Because last time we smoked together, I fell asleep."

"Good point." I carried everything to the chair and sat while packing my bowl. "You might need some after, though." I smoked in silence for a moment while she waited. "Thanks again for the balm."

"Oh." She ducked her head, cheeks flushing. "Any time."

"I'm serious. It's good shit."

"Everyone used to make fun of me for my hippie shit."

I held up the bowl in exhibit. "You *are* a hippie. Embrace it."

"Touché." She fixed her eyes on the bedspread. "Are you smoked up enough now?"

"I don't think I'll ever be." I put down the bowl. "I just found out that one of our members has been molesting his niece."

I expected her to look appalled, to cry or gasp. Instead, she flinched, wrapping her arms around herself. If I hadn't been looking, I might not have noticed. I didn't think she was even aware of her own body language. But I saw it all the same.

"Molested," she muttered. "Why do we use such benign words for such awful things? Call it like it is, Mercy. One of your members raped that little girl." She shuddered. "Which one?" she asked, her voice cold. Her eyes met mine, demanding the truth without a single word.

"Bastard." Even his name made me nauseous.

"He always gave me a weird feeling," she said. "What are you going to do?" Again, her tone lacked any emotion.

"We'll take a vote. It'll be unanimous. We'll strip him of his patch and ranking, and then remove him."

"Remove him?" She arched a skeptical eyebrow at me, her first facial expression in several long minutes.

"Yes," I said, voice hard.

"Good." She shuddered. "I don't like the way he looks at me."

"You're too old for him," I seethed.

"Maybe." She shook her head. "How old is his niece?"

"Seven? Eight? I'm not sure."

She held out a hand. "I'll take that now."

I passed the bowl and lighter over to her. "This goes without saying, but you can't repeat this. Not even to Shannon—though I'm sure Mercy's filled her in. He tells her everything."

"I appreciate," she said, holding in the smoke, "that you trusted me with this. You know, as your fake ol' lady."

I nodded. "I want to kill him now."

"So why not? I mean, isn't that a biker thing? Murder and mayhem?" She passed the bowl back to me.

"Murder and mayhem, huh?" I took a hit, my limbs calming,

my pulse slowing. "We're a club, Bree. None of us can just go around doing whatever we want."

"I think this is special circumstances, yeah?"

"You'd think," I said with a sigh. "It sure feels like it. I don't know how Ravage walked out of that house without strangling him."

Her eyes widened. "Ravage *caught* him?"

"More or less."

"And he didn't try to stop him?" Her eyes flashed.

"Like I said, there's a code—"

"Fuck the code!" She slashed a hand through the air. "He had the chance to help that little girl, and he, what, just snuck away?"

"It's complicated, Bree."

"It's pretty fucking simple, actually," she huffed.

"You're right." Bowing my head, I rested it in my hands. "You're right," I repeated. "I built this club with him. I've known him for years, and I had no idea. I know nothing."

"*No*," she said. She pulled my hands from my face. I opened my eyes. She knelt in front of me, eyes intent on mine. "You can't blame yourself for this. You didn't know. Now that you know, though, you can't just pretend it didn't happen. You can't, Mercy. Promise me. Don't let them sweep this under the rug."

"We aren't," I swore. "Ravage and I are on this. It's going to be okay." I gave her what I hoped was a reassuring smile.

"Okay for who?" she asked in a small voice, turning away.

I wondered the same.

15

NOW

The next morning, my chase resumes.

I climb onto the Softail with stiff joints and an ache in my chest. I could turn around and go back to Connecticut. Or I could head to Claudine's and pick up Bree's trail from there. Except there won't be footprints or breadcrumbs guiding me.

I ride aimlessly, pushing myself farther down 13 and withdrawing into my thoughts. I should've known better. All I've wanted for the past twenty years is to go back to the white box house with my wife and daughter. I should've known that Bree might not want the same thing. The short time we had together there was so happy, so perfect. It never occurred to me that she might feel differently. I've clung to a delusion over the past two decades.

Whatever got me through, I guess.

I pull over at the next gas station and buy a disposable cell phone and a questionable sandwich. It takes me several minutes to get the damned phone package open, even with my pocket knife. It takes another twenty while I figure out how to load the card onto the phone. It takes one bite for me to realize the sandwich was a bad idea.

I dial Ravage's cell from memory.

"There he is," he answers. "How's the road?"

I peel the bread apart and drop both halves onto the plastic wrap. "She's off," I say softly.

"Kinda had a feeling that'd happen," he says with a sigh. "Any idea where?"

"I was hoping I could pick Shannon's brain." If she's even home. While I've been away, Shannon's been working around the clock to grow her non-profit for sexual violence survivors: Shannon's Haven.

"Yeah, hang on." He lowers the phone from his ear, holding it to his chest, fabric swishing against the mic.

I listen to the creaks as he moves through his and Shannon's house. I've never set foot inside. Maybe I never will.

"Shan," he says gently. "Mercer's on the phone."

There's more static and shifting, and then I hear her voice. "It's about fucking time."

"Soon it'll be in person," I promise, guilt wringing my heart.

"Hope so. I'll haunt your ass if I don't get to see you before I die."

"She's serious," Ravage reminds me.

"Dead serious," she says. She sounds good. I've missed so much of her life, of everything. It's heartening to know at least one thing hasn't changed. "Claudine?" she asks.

"I didn't make it in time." The story of my life. Time is slipping through my fingers and it's all I can do to hold onto it. "I was wondering if you had any idea where Bree might've gone."

"I wish." She sighs. "It's been so long since I've even spoken to her."

"Try not to hold it against her," I say.

"I just want her to be okay."

"I know." I bow my head, the untouched sandwich staring me in the face. "So no ideas?"

"I know her haunts around here, Merce. Not Virginia."

"It's warm," Ravage cuts in. "Check the beaches. Hampton has a few of 'em."

"I guess that's a start." I gather my trash, itching to get back onto the road. At this rate, I won't make it into Hampton for another week.

"You'll find her," Shannon soothes. "The two of you are written in the stars."

"What if we aren't? What if this is just some clingy ex-con shit?" I tug at my hair.

"Can't be. You two had a connection right from the get go."

"It's a shame about the felony," Ravage chimes in.

"Tell me about it." I did the right thing, though—for all of us. "And tell me again about my daughter," I beg Shannon.

"I haven't seen her in a few months," she reminds me.

"I know. Tell me again." Olivia is my favorite fairytale.

She's silent for a moment. "I hired her. Trained her. Taught her everything I know about bartending. She's stubborn, like you."

I grin.

"She's got your eyes."

"Don't tease me."

"She does, though. I don't know how, but she does. And those wild curls of hers. God, you'd love her."

"I already do."

"Then get Bree and come home, Mercy."

"I'm working on it."

I tell her I love her, and then we hang up.

I hold the cell phone in my hand, tossing it a couple of inches into the air, then catching it in my palm. Every time it lands, it makes a satisfying *smack*, the weight of it dipping into my flesh for a moment, then bouncing back up.

I want to call my daughter.

I want to hear her voice. I want to hear about her life. I want to hear how much I've missed, how much she's missed me all these years.

It's selfish.

For all I know, she hasn't missed me for even a second. There's a chance Bree never even told her about me. Or she's pissed at me for being in jail when I should've been home.

I keep hoping that maybe if I bring her mother back to her, Olivia will forgive me. But maybe it won't be enough.

16

1997

I swung around the corner of the hall that led into the bar, nearly crashing into Ravage.

"You ready?" he asked.

"Not really." I glanced toward the open doors of the Chapel. "Everybody inside?"

He nodded. "As VP, you're gonna need to be the one to bring up the motion."

"I know." I squared my shoulders. "Let's get this over with." I headed toward the doors.

"I wonder if I should've given everyone a heads up," he said in a low voice as we approached.

"Nah. This is gonna be cut and dry, brother." Still, my stomach pulsed, my intestines in knots. Hard lumps sat in my belly, and not even the strongest coffee could get me going again. In a few minutes, it'd all be over. I'd betray my best friend and send him to the river.

I'd probably have to take him myself.

I strode into the Chapel, nodding at each of my brothers as I passed them. Taking my seat beside the head of the table, where Bastard always sat, I swiveled my head toward the door.

I wanted to look him in the eye from the moment he walked in.

Ravage headed toward the seat across from me, his boots thudding on the wooden floor. He pulled the chair out, its legs scraping against the wood. Then he dropped into it, lighting a cigarette. He gave me a nod.

A second later, Bastard walked in.

The air of the room changed.

It thickened, somehow, tightening the shoulders of every man sitting around the table. I'd never noticed it before. Maybe I was imagining it. Or maybe I'd been in denial. Bastard had shed his humanity a long time ago. I'd just been too wrapped up in my own pain to see it.

Every step he took reverberated throughout the room. He took his time, strolling around the table, clasping each man's shoulder the way he usually did. Gavin, our Enforcer, laid his own hand on top of Bastard's for a brief moment.

Then Bastard took his seat.

"Morning," he said, watching us out of eyes sunken into hollows. Even his appearance had transformed.

I studied him for other signs, for any hint that the boy I'd grown up with, gone to war with was still in there somewhere. He wasn't.

"Let's talk financials," Bastard said. "Mark?"

Running a hand through his long hair, Mark flipped open his ledger. "All good. We've got enough cash put aside to go for a nice long ride this month."

I swear, Bastard's eyes rippled, twin snakes shifting beneath black water.

"And our side business?" he asked, shooting a glance toward me.

Mark closed the ledger. "Not half bad. I funneled it in under donations."

"Donations for what?" Zed asked with a chuckle.

"Skid's hospital fund," Donny quipped.

Despite the tension, I smiled. Our Prospect Skid took quite the spill during an errand, ending up with road rash all down one side of his body. He was fine, minus the gnarly scarring, still raw in some places.

"That'll work," Mark said, grinning at Donny.

"Anything else?" Bastard demanded.

"You got somewhere else to be, Pres?" Donny asked.

"Bastard's got a girlfriend," Beer Can teased.

Ravage's eyes met mine across the table. My jaw tightened.

"Our VP has something he'd like to bring to the table," Ravage told them.

I looked at Bastard one final time, still hoping to find *something* there. His green eyes met mine, cold and dark. I scrubbed at my beard, stomach twisting.

I laid my palms flat on the table. "We need to vote on something," I said, voice scraping in my throat. I kept my eyes on Bastard's. "Our Sergeant-at-Arms walked in on our President . . ." I swallowed. I had to use the words. If I was going to call him out, push a vote through for his death sentence, I needed to say the words.

"You've all met his little niece Lucy at one time or another," I continued, eyes still on Bastard.

He regarded me with a twisted mouth, empty eyes, brows pinched together. His head cocked to the side, as if to say, "Try me."

"Ravage walked in on him assaulting her." I pulled in a shallow breath through my nose, struggling to keep my breathing even. Bree's words echoed in my head. "*Raping* her," I amended. "He forced a little girl to have sex with him. His own niece."

His expression didn't change.

Mutters rippled through the table, my brothers' voices raising as they all began talking at once.

"Wait," Gavin said. "Why isn't Ravage bringing this to the table? Since he *allegedly* caught Bastard."

"Because Mercy is our VP," Ravage said calmly. "I took it to our VP."

"Rather than take it up with our President?" Zed asked.

"Take it up?" Ravage scoffed. "This isn't a disagreement, brother. This is child rape."

"I know this is a lot to take in," I said, trying to redirect the conversation. I'd never needed to bring anything to the table. Usually I let Bastard run the show. He was good at it. I'd let him play me long enough. "We need to vote: Should we take Bastard down to the river?"

"Doesn't he even get to speak?" Zed demanded.

"Are you suggesting Ravage and Mercy are lying?" Donny growled.

"We don't have any protocol in place for something like this," Beer Can said.

Ravage's nostrils flared. "I want a vote."

"Oh, I already know what my vote is," Beer Can said. "I was just . . . I don't know." He bowed his head, face quivering in anger.

Bastard lit a cigarette, moving for the first time in several minutes. "So let's vote." He took a long drag. "Do I get a vote, VP? Or do I leave my two cents out of this?"

"Of course you get a vote," I told him. "This is a democracy. Even rapists get a say."

His lip curled as he laughed, a short, cocky sound. "I just want to say one thing before we vote."

I lifted a hand. "Please. Enlighten us."

"We've got a good thing going, boys," Bastard said. "A town that doesn't mind us. A bar full of bikers wearing all colors, plenty of pussy to go around."

"Be even more if we got that escort service up and running," Gavin grumbled.

"We're *not* running a brothel," Mark said with a sigh.

"Here we go again," Donny muttered.

"We've got a full table," Bastard continued. "A nice, rounded table. Ten of us. Everything running like clockwork. What happens outside these walls doesn't affect any of that."

From the foot of the table, Abraham frowned.

I pressed my palms tighter against the table. If I moved them, they'd be around Bastard's neck. Then we'd be down to a table of eight.

"What you should all be asking yourselves is, why didn't our VP and Sergeant-at-Arms confront me? Why this cloak and dagger shit?"

"We don't have a protocol in place," Beer Can reminded us.

"What are you, my fucking secretary?" Bastard growled.

"Let's vote," Ravage rumbled. "Pres, you start."

"Nay, you fucking coward. You're not getting my club," Bastard said.

"This is *our* club," I snarled, my hands curling into fists. "Yea," I said, voice resounding through the Chapel.

Beside me, Mark gave his vote. "Yea."

"Yea, you fucking scumbag," Beer Can said. He spat onto the floor.

Malcolm shifted in his seat. "I don't know," he said slowly. "Something ain't right here. I vote nay."

"Are you fucking kidding me?" Beer Can demanded. "She's a little kid, for fuck's sake!"

"Where's the proof?" Malcolm shot back. "All we have is our VP and Sergeant-at-Arms coming at us with stories."

"Well, you gave your vote," Mark said. "Abraham? What's your vote?"

Leather creaked as every River Reaper faced Abraham.

He shook his head over and over. "I'm . . . I don't know. This doesn't feel right. Malcolm is right. Nay."

"You sons of bitches," Beer Can muttered. "How can you slide this under the rug?"

Nothing was happening like it should. There shouldn't even be any debate.

I glanced at Ravage. He pressed his teeth together hard enough to shatter enamel. "Donny?" he seethed.

"Yea. Fucking yea. We don't tolerate this shit. *Yea*," he said again.

"We fucking heard you," Malcolm said under his breath.

"You wanna say that so I can hear you?" Donny demanded.

"Enough," Gavin said, folding his scarred hands on the table. "Zed, your vote."

It was the first time our Enforcer had to regain order at our table.

Zed shook his head. "I'm with Gavin and Malcolm. This is wrong. Nay."

"What's wrong," Ravage said, "is raping your own niece. A little girl. *That's* what's wrong. What the fuck is the matter with all of you?"

"Ravage," Gavin warned. "It's my vote. I vote nay.

"And we already know Ravage is all for the yea," Bastard said.

"Yea," Ravage shot back.

The man I'd grown up with, served in the military with, built a club with leaned back in his seat, smugger than I'd ever seen him. "Split table. No motion." He knocked on the table. "We're done here." He stood and stretched, yawning lazily. "I'll be in my office, if anyone wants to talk to me face to face."

He strolled out, calm as when he'd first walked in.

"I know what you're doing," Malcolm said, standing. He spat toward me. "I won't stand for it. We've all got a place here. Be happy with yours." With those last words, he stomped out.

Zed and Gavin followed him, shaking their heads.

"Abraham?" I faced the man sitting at the end of the table.

He shook his head, avoiding eye contact. Slowly, he stood, pushing his chair back. Then he filed out too.

Only Mark, Ravage, Beer Can, Donny, and I remained at the table.

"What the fuck just happened?" Ravage growled, voicing all of our thoughts out loud.

17

NOW

I cross the Hampton city line just as the sky unloads. Torrents of rain spill down on me, soaking through my clothing, cloaking the road in front of me. I veer to the side of the road, the Softail wavering. It splashes through a puddle, dousing me with mud. Then I finally stop.

It's a bad omen.

I pull out my cell phone, thankful that it was protected by the leather of my cut. I almost didn't wear my club colors, almost left the piece of leather behind. But come whatever may, I'll always be a River Reaper. I built this club with my bare hands, breaking my back right alongside Sebastian.

I don't expect Ravage and the others to let me back in. Not after the stunt I pulled. I think Ravage understands, but the rest of them won't.

I'm not even sure I understand.

Chasing a woman who doesn't even want me across the country is desperate, even kind of creepy. She told me to go away, so I should.

I can't.

I made vows, vows I don't intend to break. For better or worse.

For present wife or runaway wife. In the Disney movie version of this story, I'll find her on the beach and we'll run into each other's arms, share a Nicholas Sparks kiss in the rain.

Yeah, I've seen *The Notebook*. Even in max, we're allowed to watch movies. I haven't seen anything recent, though. I've got a lot of catching up to do.

I dial Claudine's number, fingers slipping on the keypad from the rain.

"Hello?" she asks, her voice smoky and sleepy.

"I'm in Hampton," I tell her.

"She's gone," she warns me.

"I'm not going to stop looking."

"I already checked the beaches, Mercy."

I stare out into the rain, at the pine boughs waving over the road. "I've got to check again."

"I know you do." She sighs. "I tried."

"You owe me nothing," I say. "I just need one more favor."

"Anything," she says quickly. "This is all my fault."

"Listen to me, Claudine. None of this is your fault. It's all on me. You can let go." I don't often dwell on regrets, but Claudine is one do-over I wish I could get.

For a long moment, she says nothing. I can only imagine what her shoes feel like. Too tight, but also lonely. The club was all she had and now, because of me, she has nothing. If they let me back in, I'll try to get her back into their good graces.

It's time for all of us to stop living in the past.

Especially if I can't find Bree.

18

1997

The stairs rose in front of me, the steps steeper than when I'd descended them. My shoulders drooped under the weight of it all: the little girl, my ended friendship with Bastard, the split vote. The last thing I'd expected was for any of us to vote nay. What the fuck was wrong with my brothers? How could they seriously believe that Ravage and I were trying to take over the MC?

I'd never been interested in being President. I hadn't even wanted to be Vice President. I stomped up the stairs, blood boiling. I'd only taken the VP patch at Bastard's insistence.

"You're the only one I can do this with," he'd said.

It was all bullshit. Everything. From the government I'd fought for to the club I'd built. I'd just been lying to myself.

In a world so masked, I couldn't tell what was real anymore. I had no idea what was going to happen to my club, the only thing I had left. If we couldn't come to a majority vote, nothing would change. Bastard would remain President, would continue molesting Lucy until someone caught him.

Or killed him.

I hesitated at the top of the stairs. I could do it. I could save that little girl. With a knife or a gun or my bare hands. I could choke the life out of him until those dead eyes went dull. Problem solved.

And then I'd have no more club.

I'd have no protection.

I'd go to jail, spend the rest of my life in prison with no allies.

All for breaking club code.

The very thing I loved would be the very thing to destroy me.

I trudged down the hall. There was no solution. Somehow, I had to convince my brothers that Ravage and I weren't trying to take anything over. Someone else could be President and VP, for all I cared. All I'd ever wanted was a simple life.

I tapped my knuckles against the door to my room, then pushed it open. "Hello," I called out, peering into the dark. The only light came from a *Friends* episode on TV.

"Hi," Bree said, her throat clogged, her nose full of sniffles.

I flipped on the light.

She sat huddled on the bed, red eyes tracking me as I crossed the room. "Sorry," she whispered.

"For what?" My hands hung at my sides, joints pulsing with hot pain. My useless hands. I couldn't remove Bastard, couldn't comfort Bree.

"I'll go . . . somewhere else." She gestured to nothing, then scooped up the pile of used tissues in front of her.

"Stay?" I remained where I stood, afraid that if I moved any closer, she'd bolt.

She shrugged.

"Want to talk about it?"

She sucked in a shaky breath. "I don't know what I'm going to do," she whispered.

I knew the feeling. "Maybe we can figure it out together." I took slow steps, then sat in the chair I always sat in when we talked.

"I don't think so." She gave me a watery smile. "But thanks."

I nodded toward the dresser. "Want to smoke?" I knew I did.

"I can't."

"You're working tonight?" I stretched toward the dresser, contorting my torso as I reached to open the top drawer. "I don't think Shannon will care."

She shook her head, her bangs falling into her eyes. "I'm pregnant." Fresh tears streaked her cheeks, dripping onto her paisley skirt.

I froze, hands in midair above the drawer. My ribs protested. I withdrew back into my seat, facing her. I needed to say something. I couldn't think of a single comforting word. I wrapped a hand around my chin, rubbing at the stubble. She looked so small on that bed, so fragile and alone.

My sweet friend, who'd made me magic balm and listened to my troubles. She'd been in trouble all along, and there was nothing I could do for her.

I exhaled. "Does the father know?"

She paled. "He can never know. Never."

I ran a hand through my hair, putting the pieces together. Her strong reaction when I told her about little Lucy. Her tendency for being two seconds away from bolting. Her avoiding all men —*almost* all men.

"He raped you," I said, meeting her eyes.

She nodded once.

My jaw hardened. The pain faded from my limbs, adrenaline pumping through me. "I'll kill him. Tell me who he is, Bree. I will kill him."

She shook her head. "I can't."

Standing, I went to her. I dropped down on my knees in front of the bed, taking her hands. "He doesn't deserve your protection."

"It's not him I'm protecting," she said softly.

My eyes dropped to her stomach, to the tiny bump I'd somehow missed. God, I was so stupid.

"My daughter," she said. "If I do anything to hold him responsible—if I report him, if I let you kill him—she'll walk around with his stain on her. I want better for her."

My eyes burned, my throat tightening. This tiny woman held more strength inside of her than I could've ever guessed. "Bree," I whispered, stroking her hands and shaking my head.

"It's okay." She twined her fingers with mine. "I'll figure something out."

I swallowed. "Marry me."

Her mouth twitched. "What?"

I sucked in a deep breath in an attempt to steady my shaking hands. "Marry me," I repeated. "Be my real ol' lady. I'll take care of both of you. Your daughter will have a father, and no one will ever have to know otherwise."

Her eyebrows knit together. "Mercy, I can't."

"Is it me?" I brushed hair out of my face. "Did I read this wrong? I thought maybe we had a connection, but if I'm wrong, I'm sorry."

Her shoulders tightened. "You're not wrong." She looked away, down at our still entwined hands.

"Then what is it?"

"I can't marry you," she said to our hands, "because I'm fourteen."

"You're eighteen," I said. "That's what you told me. And Shannon."

She peeked up at me from under wet lashes. "I lied."

I brushed my thumb across the top of her hand. "I get it. You did what you had to do." I glanced around the room, as if the paintings and curtains would give me the answers I needed.

Everything was so completely FUBAR.

I'd been pining after a fourteen-year-old. I was just as vile as Bastard.

Tears splotched her skirt. Several dripped onto our hands. "I'll figure something out," she repeated.

I took a deep breath. I could put my feelings for her aside. I could do that for her. I needed to be able to do something for her. She'd done everything for me. She'd listened, she'd *seen* me and my pain, and she'd even tried to help. Not even my brothers had done those things for me.

"I'll marry you anyway." I stood, keeping our hands joined, and sat next to her.

She looked at me like I had three heads. "How? You'd need my parents' consent."

"So, we'll get their consent." I tipped her chin up. "It's going to be okay. I've got you."

"My parents don't know anything. They don't even know where I am. I ran away."

"I figured," I said dryly. "We'll call them, invite them to lunch somewhere that isn't a strip club. I'll clean up. I'll take full responsibility."

"They'll hate you," she said.

I shrugged. "Who doesn't?"

She dipped her head. "Oh no. I didn't even ask you about the vote."

I scoffed. "Isn't important."

"It is too. How did it go?"

"As bad as it possibly could." I gave her hand a gentle squeeze. "It's going to be okay," I repeated.

She bowed her head. "How? There's no way out of this." She withdrew her hand from mine, waving. "If I stay here, I'll never be able to sleep. Not with Bastard skulking around, waiting for my daughter in the shadows." She shuddered.

My blood ran cold.

Standing from the bed, I paced. More of Phee's paintings decorated the walls, each more depressing than the last. I couldn't give Bree any of the things she deserved: happiness, safety, peace of mind. But I could at least give her what she wanted for her daughter. And I could do everything in my power to keep Bastard away from the three of us.

I stopped in front of her, bent down on one knee. "Bree," I said, taking her hand again. I paused. "What's your last name?"

"Vidales," she supplied.

"Bree Vidales," I said. "Will you marry me?"

"This is insane."

"I'll be a perfect gentleman," I promised.

"I've got deja vu."

"For all intents and purposes, I'll be your husband. I'll be your daughter's father. I'll fix the club and get rid of Bastard. I'll buy you happier paintings."

She laughed, wiping away her tears with the back of her other hand. "Okay."

"So you'll marry me?"

"Yes."

I stood, and she straightened on the bed. Throwing her arms around my neck, she pulled me in for a hug.

"Thank you," she whispered.

"I'm going to go find someone to officiate," I said. "You call your parents."

She pulled away from me. "We're doing this *now*?"

"If you want. I just thought we'd tell the club *after*."

She gaped at me. "You mean, you're not going to tell them the truth?"

"This is the truth. We've been dating for weeks. We're madly in love. We're going to have a baby, so we got married."

"You make it sound so nice," she said, tone wistful.

"It can be." I caught a flyaway strand of her hair between two of my fingers. I smoothed it into the rest of her hair.

"What if they find out?"

"What's there to find out? You're eighteen, remember?" I grinned.

"I don't want to get anyone in trouble."

"You won't."

She nodded, head dipped. "All right. I'll call them."

"I'll go round up a priest." I stepped back, unable to take my eyes off her. In another life, we might've had the perfect story. I had no idea what it felt like to fall in love, but I knew I was doing the right thing. I liked her. Respected her. Cared about her. And I was in a position to help her.

Shannon was going to lose her mind when I told her we were married. I could already hear her telling me she'd told me so. It hurt no one to let all of them think it was all that simple.

Love. Marriage. Babies.

All the things I should have, but couldn't ever let myself hope for.

"See you soon," I said.

"See you." She lifted a hand.

I waited another moment, mentally taking a snapshot of her kneeling on the bed, her messy hair hanging around her face, her eyes full of hope.

At least I'd solved one problem.

* * *

I caught up with Phee by the Freihofer outlet. She had exactly one ring for sale, a sterling silver ring with a huge turquoise stone. It screamed Bree. I paid for it and tucked it into my pocket, then headed toward Cara's, the diner where I was supposed to meet Bree, her parents, and the Justice of the Peace I'd hired.

I stepped inside Cara's, nerves crawling with both my usual pain and my newfound anxiety. I'd told her I didn't care if her parents hated me, but I wanted them to like me—for her sake. Even I knew that no parents in their right mind would approve of us. I'd be lucky if they didn't call the cops and have me arrested.

It was a long shot and a half.

I hoped that, because we were in public, they'd sign their consent without making a scene.

I spotted the back of Bree's head and headed over to their

table. "Hi," I said as I drew near. I shook hands with the JP, then held a hand out to Bree's father.

Mr. Vidales eyed me with obvious mistrust. "You're twice her age," he said.

Beside him, Mrs. Vidales glared at me openly. She turned to Bree. "Is this a joke?"

"No, Mama." Bree stirred her coffee a little too hard.

I dropped my hand and took a seat beside her. I glanced at the mug of hot liquid. "Is that safe?" I asked in a low voice.

"Safe for everyone here," she said between her teeth.

I cleared my throat. "I'm Mercer," I told her parents. "It's really nice to finally meet you."

"It's obvious what's going on here," Mrs. Vidales said in a clipped tone. She shot a pointed look at the JP.

"You're pregnant," Mr. Vidales said accusingly. "You run away, shack up with a biker, and get yourself knocked up." He shook his head in disgust. "And now you want our permission to marry the devil."

"I just want to do the right thing," I said, touching Bree's shoulder.

She relaxed a little, but her cheeks remained pink. "Please, Daddy. Mama. This is what I want."

Her mother scoffed.

The JP shifted uncomfortably. "Do you all need a minute?"

"No," Bree and I said at the same time.

She turned back to her parents. "Please."

They exchanged glances.

"We'll sign," her mother said.

"But that's all," her father continued. He nodded to the form on the table. "After we sign, we're walking out of here. You get nothing else from us. Do you hear me? We're so disappointed in you, Bree."

Her teeth sank into her lip. She picked up her spoon, resuming her stirring. I rubbed her shoulder, wishing I could do more to spare her from this. In a perfect world, she'd feel safe telling her parents and the world the truth. The bad guy would rot in jail, and no one would look twice at Bree's baby. The world was not perfect, though. She lifted her chin. "Fine," she said, voice unwavering.

The JP pushed the form across the table, pointing to where each of us were supposed to sign. Before the ink was even dry, her parents stood and walked out of the diner. They didn't even look back.

"I can give you a moment," the JP offered.

"No," Bree said, blinking away tears. "Just do it." She turned toward me in the booth, taking my hands.

"I've got you," I whispered while the JP started.

She nodded.

Neither of us heard the words he said. We sat, hands joined, eyes locked. When it was time to exchange rings, I slipped the turquoise piece onto her finger. Tears fell from her eyes, her smile lighting up the entire diner.

"How did you know?" she asked.

The JP pronounced us husband and wife, and I gave her a quick kiss on the cheek.

She lifted her chin. "Thank you," she whispered.

"Any time." I paid the JP, who hurried out of the diner as if the whole place was on fire. I turned back to my wife. "Where to now?"

19

NOW

I start with Buckroe, taking Claudine's car to the beach to keep the rain off me. The last thing my joints need is another soaking. Even though I'm afraid, I'm also hoping I'll find Bree here and she'll come back to Claudine's with me. I know Claudine said she looked, but maybe she didn't look hard enough. I'd recognize the back of Bree's head anywhere. Claudine wouldn't, no matter how well she meant.

Even as the rain slows to a steady drizzle, the beach remains empty. I walk up and down the coast, hoping to catch a glimpse of her in the water or huddled underneath an umbrella.

No Bree.

I hit Grandview next. It's less of a beach and more of a giant nature preserve. It's not exactly Bree's place, but there's a good chance she might've drifted this way, if only for all of the shells. My boots crunch over dozens of them as I comb the place. There's really no point. Even if there are hundreds of acres to explore, there's no one here.

The place is as void as my chances of winning her back.

If I ever even had her.

By the time I get to Outlook Beach, the rain has almost

completely stopped, the sun peeking out of the clouds now and then. A few people come out of whatever shelter they ducked into during the downpour, but it's easy to scan through the sparse crowd.

No Bree.

I could take Claudine's car and try Virginia Beach, but I've got a feeling it's just as much of a hopeless task.

She's gone.

I take the long way back to Claudine's, using her GPS to find the most time-consuming route. I blast the heat on my still wet clothes and damp joints, and think.

Maybe it's time to accept that Bree really wants nothing to do with me. Once upon a time, I was a hero in her story, but not *the* hero. Not her hero. If things were different, maybe we really could've had a chance. If I'd been ten years younger. If she'd been ten years older. If no one had traumatized her. If I hadn't put everything else before her and Olivia.

If, if, if.

I can't count the what ifs anymore. All I can do is respect her wishes. Move forward. Let her go.

It's the last thing I really want to do, but I've got no choice.

I pull into Claudine's parking spot and climb out of the car, my joints stiff and screaming. I wish I had some of Bree's balm, but I'll have to settle for some store bought shit that isn't nearly strong enough. That and some of Beer Can's weed.

I limp inside, babying my right ankle, the tendons limp and useless. I collapse onto the couch.

Claudine rushes to my side. "I'm so sorry, Mercy." She packs baggies of ice all over my joints and brings one of the pens to my lips.

I take a deep toke and exhale smoke at the ceiling. "It is what it is." I sigh.

"What's next? I can take tomorrow off work. We can—"

I hold up a hand. "Tomorrow I'm going back to Connecticut."

"But Mercy—"

I shake my head. An ice pack falls from behind my neck, landing on the couch, the cubes rattling. "I need to go home. My daughter needs me." My eyes burn. I don't know what I'll tell Olivia. She doesn't know the truth. I don't know how to explain any of this—especially why I didn't bring her mother back to her.

I take another hit, dulling everything.

"I've already made up the guest bedroom for you," Claudine says softly. "You're welcome here as long as you need."

"I'm leaving tomorrow," I say again, with finality. "It's time to move on."

PART III

THE BOHEMIAN AND THE BIKER

20

1997

Bree

I sat in a chair in the back parking lot of The Wet Mermaid, my left hand on my belly. The silver glinted in the overhead light, but I only had eyes for the turquoise stone. I still couldn't believe any of it. Mercy's proposal. How he somehow knew I'd been eyeing that ring for weeks. Despite Phee always cutting me a break, I'd never be able to afford it. Not on my under the table wages.

Not with a baby on the way.

She was a girl. I knew it like Mercy knew that ring was meant for me. The obstetrician I'd seen a few days after our diner wedding told me I was only about eight weeks—miles away from being able to tell in an ultrasound—but I knew.

Sometimes, you just know.

Like I knew I was safe with Mercy.

"Here," Shannon said, stepping outside and handing me a cup of herbal tea. The steam rose into the cold dark air. Inside, music shook the walls, but outside it was quiet. Outside I could sit and rest my feet. I could avoid people's curious looks as they tried to decide whether I'd gained weight and they shouldn't say anything, or if I was pregnant and they should congratulate me. The news hadn't spread outside the club, apparently.

Not yet, anyway. Soon everyone would be talking about Mercy's very pregnant, very young looking wife. It was the lesser of two evils, but that didn't make me have to like the talk that came with it.

"Thanks." I wrapped my hands around the mug.

She ran her fingers through my hair, separating strands and braiding them. "I'm still mad I wasn't invited," she teased, "but I'm so freakin' happy for you two. I can't believe he didn't tell me!"

I smiled. Even though I hated lying to everyone—especially Shannon—it was a comfortable lie. Like a fairytale. If I tried hard enough, I could pretend we really were in love. Every time I put my hand on my belly, I pretended she really was his. Eventually, I'd believe it.

"And I'm going to be an aunt!" Shannon beamed. "You cannot even fathom how spoiled that little baby is going to be. Especially with all the tension around here? Everyone's going to need something to love on."

I nodded somberly. We'd only been married a week, and nothing really changed. I barely saw him. He was always coming and going. The few nights he did sleep in our room, he took the floor.

A perfect gentleman, like he'd said.

I wanted to tell him he didn't have to do that, that it didn't matter anymore. My parents had signed me away. We were married. No one would bat an eye if we shared a bed. I didn't care. Besides, it'd be nice to have someone nearby. The nights were always the hardest for me. No matter how tired I was, my brain always decided to replay every moment of the worst event of my life in sharp detail. It was so vivid, I felt the cold tiles of the girls' locker room shower pressing into my back. I always spent most of the night trying to remind myself that I was miles away from that teacher, that school. I was safe.

But lonely.

"Don't worry," Shannon soothed. "Everything will smooth over. Mercy and Todd've been talking to the guys who voted nay."

"Todd?" I repeated, the name unfamiliar.

"Oh." She chuckled. "Ravage. I think I'm the only one who calls him Todd." She blushed, a lovely color that accented her brown eyes and blonde hair.

I pictured a little girl with her coloring and my bird bones. Even though there was no way my baby would look like Mercy or his sister, I could pretend.

"Anyway, it'll all be okay. The table will come to a consensus. Bastard won't live long enough to see your baby. That little girl will be . . ." She sighed. "Well, she'll be free."

I pictured a little girl with Mercy's dark hair and eyes, his olive skin. She'd get my pin straight hair. Shannon could teach me how to French braid and I'd braid her hair every night after her bath.

It was probably sick to paint these pictures for myself, but hope for the future was all I had.

The door banged open. Mercy, Ravage, and the rest of the MC shot out of the club. As if they'd rehearsed, they started their bikes. The roar of engines drowned out my thoughts, cutting off further conversation. Motorcycle after motorcycle pulled out of the parking lot. As Mercy rolled past us, he gave me a stricken look.

"I'll call you," he promised.

Then they were gone.

"What was that?" I asked, setting the mug down and standing.

"I don't know." Shannon stared in the direction they'd gone.

"Mercy looked . . . I don't even know," I said.

"Ravage, too." She bit her lip, then glanced down at her watch. "It's almost time to close up. Let's go inside and wait." She grabbed the mug and put an arm around my shoulders, leading me back in.

Thankfully it was a weeknight. We had the place closed at 1:00 a.m. and cleaned up by 1:30. Shannon and I sat in the empty bar, our eyes glued to the phone. We chatted here and there, but mostly we waited for Mercy's call.

The phone finally rang at three.

She lifted it from the receiver and handed it to me.

Blinking, I took it from her. "Hello?"

"Hey," Mercy said, his voice mournful. "How're you doing?"

"I'm fine. What's going on?"

Static crackled on the line as he took a deep breath. "Bastard is dead."

My eyes shot to Shannon's. "You took another vote?"

"No." Silence stretched between us, the word gaining weight the longer he hesitated.

"Mercy?" I prodded. I glanced at Shannon again, my heart thumping against my ribs. "You didn't . . . Did you?"

"No," he said again. "It was Cliff."

"Cliff?" I struggled to remember who was who. "The one who loves Michael Bublé?"

"You're thinking of Abraham. Cliff is Bastard's son," Mercy said.

"His son?" I shook my head. "I thought he was only seventeen."

"Eighteen now. He walked in on Bastard and he didn't hesitate. He was arrested. They got him red-handed. Literally."

I touched my stomach. "So what now?" I whispered.

"We took a vote," he said. "I'm President." He sounded disgusted. "We've got to find him a lawyer. I doubt anyone can get him off, though. He's done for."

I rubbed circles into my belly as if soothing a child. "But Bastard is dead."

"Yes."

Shannon's eyes widened.

"Good," I said. "I'm sorry about Cliff, but ... good."

"His life is ruined," Mercy said, his voice breaking. "It should've been me."

"You couldn't, though," I reminded him. "The rules."

He scoffed. "The rules. All the good they've done."

"What do you mean?"

"The half that voted nay walked, Bree. I've got a half-empty table and the mess of the century in my lap. The men who were my brothers started their own MC: Bastard Brothers. Just like that," he said, snapping his fingers. "Everything's upside down."

Shannon scooted closer to me, pressing her ear near the phone. "Where's Ravage?"

"Tell her Ravage is in one piece," Mercy said. "He's my VP now."

"I heard him," she said before I could parrot the information. "I need a drink."

"Where did the rest of the club go?" I asked. I didn't really care. All I cared about were the basics: Bastard was gone and Mercy was safe. That was all that mattered. Everything was going to be better with Bastard was dead.

Cliff was just collateral damage.

The little girl was safe, and my little girl would be safe, too.

"It's so late, Bree. We'll talk more in the morning," he promised. "Go get some rest."

"Are you coming home?" I asked, already knowing the answer.

"I'm going to hang out at the police station for a while, see if I can visit Cliff. He might be eighteen, but he's still only a kid. A kid who just did us a huge favor, and ruined his own life." He sighed again. "I'll see you later."

Then he hung up.

I lowered my hand from my ear and stared at the receiver.

"Bastard is dead?" Shannon asked, taking the phone from me and hanging it up.

I nodded.

"Come on," she said, standing. "You can stay in my room tonight. No sense in sleeping in an empty bed."

I forced a smile. I appreciated that she looked out for me,, but wished it was Mercy taking me to bed instead.

* * *

Even though I knew Mercy had a lot on his hands, I got the feeling that he used his new responsibilities to avoid me. I knew he cared, I'd long felt something between us, but the second I told him my age, he couldn't get far enough from me.

I spent my afternoons and evenings helping Shannon in The Wet Mermaid. She still thought I was eighteen, so she started teaching me how to make drinks.

"Bree, make Beer Can an Old Fashioned," she said late one night.

I did everything exactly how she taught me, then passed it over the bar to him.

He took a sip, grimacing as he swallowed. "What did you do to it?" he choked out.

From then on, Shannon kept me far away from the bar.

Even though I spent most of my time surrounded by other people, my loneliness grew almost as quickly as my baby. The only person who truly knew me was far away.

I waited up for him, watching *The Golden Girls* on TV Land and replaying our first kiss. He was supposed to be my husband, but he acted more like my guardian. A guardian I barely saw.

The door creaked open and Mercy eased inside. He jumped when he saw me, breasts and belly practically busting out of the silky nightgown I'd bought just for him. "You're awake."

I took a deep breath, and patted the bed beside me. He sat down in the chair. That goddamn chair. I wanted to break it into a hundred pieces. I couldn't believe in fairytales when my happy ending kept evading me.

"Are you up to talking?" he asked, glancing at the time on our alarm clock. 3:55 a.m.

I stifled a yawn and nodded, pulling the blankets up around me.

"I've been sitting on my VA comp," he said. "I've got more than enough to buy a house." His eyes met mine and, for the first time in months, I saw something other than duty in there. Hope. He looked hopeful. "We could get a two-bedroom, put together a nursery for her." He smiled at my belly.

I wanted the story I told myself to be real, so I agreed. We bought a house, a box-shaped white Cape Cod in Watertown. Together we picked out colors for the nursery, spending an entire afternoon painting and arranging furniture. I lifted my brush to tidy up the trim, accidentally swiping dusty cornflower blue across the tip of my nose.

"You've got a little something," Mercy said with a laugh, leaning in with a handkerchief. He patted at my nose, his gaze intent.

"Did you get it?" I asked, my face tipped up toward him.

He lowered his arm. His eyes softened. "Yes."

Our chests rose and fell, bringing us closer together. I prayed silently. This was it. It had to be. *Make my story come true.* He swallowed, shoulders stiff.

"Bree," he whispered. Not a plea. A halt.

"We're married," I insisted.

He stepped away.

"Damn you, why are you avoiding me?" I tossed my paintbrush onto the tarp and planted my hands on my hips.

"I'm not," he promised.

"Then kiss me." I closed the space between us and put my hands on his shoulders.

A ripple ran through his body. "Bree," he warned again.

"Kiss me!" I stood on my tiptoes, my belly brushing against his stomach.

He placed his hands on each of my arms and eased me away from him. "You're too young."

I laughed, pointing at my stomach. "Too young? I think that no longer applies here."

He pressed the palms of his hands together and brought them to his lips. "Bree," he said again, this time a sigh.

"So, what, we're just going to play house? What's the point in even being married?" I spun toward the window. The room grew hotter every second. I didn't know what we'd been thinking, painting in August. It'd probably all peel off before drying, anyway.

It was just a waste.

He stood behind me, resting a hand on my shoulder. "I'm not playing at anything," he said.

I opened my mouth to argue when the first wave ripped through me. My knees buckled. I grabbed the windowsill for support.

"What's wrong?" he asked, wrapping his arms around me. He led me to the chair we'd picked out for rocking and nursing her.

I breathed in through my nose, out through my mouth the way the book had said to. It'd missed one important thing to expect, though: the pain.

He still only had the Softail, so he called Shannon to come get us. Time melted away, both dragging and flying. Contractions wracked me for hours until finally, *finally* I heard her cries.

"Hi," I whispered, tears dripping from my cheeks onto hers until I couldn't tell whose tears were whose. "Hi Olivia."

"Hi Olivia," Mercy cooed. He brushed my hair back from my face and pressed his lips to my forehead. "You did it," he whispered.

The nurse smiled at us. "Bree, I have to clean you up now. Do you want your father to step out?"

"He's not my father," I said, suppressing a laugh. Poor Mercy didn't look *that* old. I glanced up at him. His face was pale, frozen.

The nurse frowned at us. "Is he the father?" she asked, her voice taking on a scolding tone.

"He's my husband," I said.

Her face hardened. "I see." She swept out of the room.

"Mercy?" I whispered, reaching for him.

"It's all right." He threaded his fingers through mine, giving them a squeeze. "Can I hold her?"

"Of course," I said. "She's your daughter."

Pride shone through his face. I passed her to him, marveling at how he wrapped her in his arms, cuddling her close. We were in good hands. I'd made the right decision. It really would be okay.

He rocked her in his arms, singing The Rolling Stones' "Wild Horses" in a soft timbre I'd never heard him use. He shook his head, blinking tears away, and my heart could've burst.

Then someone knocked on the door. The nurse returned, with a hospital social worker and two police officers in tow.

"It's okay," Mercy said, passing Olivia back to me.

All I could do was watch as they cuffed him and took him away.

21

NOW

Bree

People rush by me with various suitcases in tow. A woman tugs one behind her, its wheels catching on the edge of a fatigue mat for a moment before bouncing, righting itself. She hurries away, barely even noticing.

I've been sitting in this airport for hours today. It's a small airport, with barely any departures or arrivals. I couldn't book a flight online if I wanted to, and there aren't even any flights that go straight to Connecticut. The closest is Philadelphia. I'd have to hop on another plane.

It's an option.

It's not *the* option, though.

I consider the departures again. It's a short list, one I've memorized: Philadelphia, Charlotte, Atlanta. Head back north or go farther south.

I just don't know if I have enough cash on me.

The only way to find out is to walk up to that counter and try to buy a ticket. Instead, I sit. I watch. I wait.

What I'm waiting for, I don't know.

A sign, maybe? If I still had tarot cards, I'd pull them out. All I have is the bag I brought to Claudine's and the clothes I'm wearing. I study the toes of my boots, a pair Claudine bought me. Out of guilt, I suppose. But the past is in the past, where it needs to stay.

I just don't know where the future lies.

I suppose no one does.

Another woman walks by with a little girl in tow. The child has dark curls and wide brown eyes. She looks just like Olivia did. My heart constricts in my chest. My baby—I miss her more than anything. She's a million times better off without me. I know that down to my soul. I didn't deserve her, and she deserved far better than me.

Which is why I need to stay away.

Standing, I stretch the last few hours out of my muscles. Then I walk up to the counter.

"Can I help you, ma'am?" His Southern accent is thick. Virginia is weird like that. In some towns in this state, everyone has a nowhere accent. Then there are places like Newport News.

"I need a flight to Charlotte, please." I place my hands on the counter, splaying my fingers. A dozen rings glint in the florescent light. If I have to, I'll find the nearest pawn shop and unload some of them. Most of them mean nothing to me, anyway. They're just decoration.

He taps some keys on his computer, the clacking soothing my frayed nerves. "The next flight out is for 8:11 this evening, ma'am. Will that do?"

"Please," I confirm. He tells me the price and I reach into my bag for my wallet. As I undo the button and reach for the crumpled bills, I stop dead. Everything moves in slow motion. I lift my left hand, lips parted, pain blossoming in my chest.

The stone.

The turquoise stone.

In the ring Mercy gave me.

It's gone.

The gasp steals all the air from my lungs. I wheeze, eyes still locked on the now empty ring. Like the stone will just reappear. I turn in a slow circle, stooped, gaze sweeping across the floor.

It's not there.

I run back to the bench I'd been sitting on, dropping to my hands and knees. I find a gum wrapper, a dime, a plastic something. No stone.

It's gone.

Tears rush down my cheeks. I drag my shaking fingers along the floor again and again, coming up empty.

"Ma'am?" A wary security guard looms over me. "Are you all right?"

I blink up at him, sobbing like a child. "It's gone," I tell him.

His hand drops to the walkie on his belt. "What's gone?"

"My ring—the stone," I gasp, ducking under the bench. "Help me look."

He crawls alongside me, halfheartedly patting the floor for the stone we both know isn't there. "Have you retraced your steps?" he asks.

I shake my head, tears dripping onto the tiles. "I've been sitting on this bench all day," I sob. "I wouldn't know where to start."

"It's all right," he says, patting my shoulder awkwardly.

But it isn't. Everything is miles away from *all right*. It's all wrong.

I back out of the bench cave, then sit up on my knees. "I never should've left," I tell him.

"Is there someone I can call for you?" he asks, blue eyes full of compassion—something rare up north where I come from.

"I think this is my sign." I brush at my tears, but they keep coming.

"Your sign?" His mouth quirks.

"I never should've left," I say again. "Do you think twenty-one years is too late?"

He shrugs. "My mama always said better late than never."

"Your mama was a smart lady." I stand, brushing my skirt. I won't ever find that stone. I probably won't even find Mercy.

But I know where to start looking.

22

1997

Bree

The investigation took months. Because we were married, the police couldn't hold Mercy for long, but it loomed over us.

I rocked Olivia in the nursery, glancing at the clock on the wall. She'd fallen asleep hours ago. I didn't want to move. If I moved, I'd jinx it all.

The squeal of the front door opening echoed up the stairs. Mercy's footfalls grew slower as he climbed, his steps heavy. He leaned against the frame of the door. "Hey," he whispered.

"Hey," I whispered back.

"She out?"

I nodded, peeking down at her. She looked nothing like I'd imagined. She had wide brown eyes, and curls I'd never be able to brush without tangling. Her skin was fair, almost porcelain. There was no hint of the story I'd told myself throughout the past eight months.

"Can we talk?" Mercy whispered.

I laid her down in her crib and tiptoed out of the room,

closing the door behind me. In the tiny hall, we were forced to stand so near each other, my heartbeat matched his.

He pressed his hands together, skull rings catching the sunlight that streamed in. Exhaling, he closed his eyes. "The lawyer says," he began, keeping his eyes closed, "they wouldn't normally have a case, because we're married."

"But?" I pressed.

"But that nurse knows the DA, and she's got it out for me."

"Us," I corrected.

He shrugged, and his eyes popped open. "Because we weren't married when Olivia was conceived, they're prosecuting it as statutory rape."

I sagged against the wall. "What if I testify?"

He shook his head. "Doesn't matter. You were under the age of consent."

"What if we draw blood, prove Olivia isn't yours?" I begged.

He froze.

"I didn't mean it like that," I said quickly. "I just meant, if they knew we've never even had sex, none of it will matter."

"And then?" He crossed his arms.

I rubbed my lips together. "And then we'll all just have to live with the truth."

"No," he insisted. "That's not what you want."

"I also don't want you to go to prison!"

"It's okay." He touched my chin. "It's actually better this way."

I jerked my face away. "What the hell is that supposed to mean?"

"It means someone's got to watch out for Cliff in there."

I frowned. "So you're going to let this happen," I said slowly, "so that you can cover the club's ass?"

"I'm doing it for you, too. For Olivia. This is what we agreed on."

"I *never* wanted you to go to jail."

"We both knew it was a possibility. You had to have known,

deep down, Bree." He ran a thumb along my jaw. "It's the only way."

Tears burned my eyes. "You can fight this. We can."

"No," he insisted. "It's better this way for everyone: Olivia, Cliff, the club. I've got this."

"What if it's not better for me?" My hands curled into fists at my sides. I wanted to hurl them at him, to bruise his chest the way he was bruising my heart. "What am I supposed to do without you?"

"Take care of our daughter," he said.

"She's not your daughter," I lobbed at him.

He flinched. "So you did mean it."

I lifted my chin. "I'll tell everyone. Olivia is not Mercy's. Neither of us belong to you."

He stepped back, shaking his head. "No," he whispered.

"You can't just decide for us."

"I already did. I signed a confession. I'm supposed to turn myself in tomorrow morning."

My lips quivered. "You're not doing this for us," I said. "You're doing this for the club—the club that fucked you over!"

He said nothing, only regarded me with guarded eyes, his emotions concealed from me.

"I want a divorce," I said, panic rising in my chest. Tears tracked burn marks down my cheeks, so hot, they could set everything they touched on fire.

"Do whatever you want," he said, turning away. "Once I'm inside, I won't be able to contest it." With his back to me, he marched down the stairs. A moment later, the door opened, then slammed shut.

I fell to my knees in the hallway, weeping.

I lost track of how long I lay there, curled into a ball, my limbs aching. Just like that, he'd given everything up. And for what? For some insane sense of loyalty to Bastard's son? I couldn't understand it. Olivia and I needed him with us, not locked up and forgotten. Once he surrendered, I'd have to tell everyone the truth. I wouldn't be able to work at The Wet Mermaid anymore. I'd have no job, no way to take care of our daughter. *My* daughter.

Fresh tears dampened the carpet beneath me.

I cried until I was empty, until Olivia's soft cries reminded me that I had my own responsibilities. Fuck him.

I stepped into the nursery, lifting her from her crib and bringing her to my breast. I didn't need him to take care of us.

I just needed *him*.

I shook my head, shaking the thought away. I didn't need anyone. I'd figure something out.

I looked down at my daughter, silently promising her I'd do whatever it took. And then her eyes opened, eyes that—despite the odds—reminded me of his.

Mercy.

It was like she was begging me to change my mind, to keep us a family. And she was right. If he could make such a sacrifice for the greater good, I could suck it up and support him from the outside. Somehow, it'd all work out. It'd be okay.

As soon as Olivia finished, I tucked her into her stroller and grabbed her diaper bag. Then we set off down the hill, toward the club house.

By the time we got there, the night had risen, with clouds so dark I couldn't see the stars. I pushed the stroller into the club, heading straight for the bar.

Shannon glanced up at me, doing a double take. Her eyes widened with shock. "Oh, no," she murmured.

"What?" I demanded, whirling toward the stairs.

"Bree," she pleaded. "Don't go up there."

"Watch your niece." I stomped up the stairs, my legs heavy with dread. I already knew what I'd find. I just needed to see with my own two eyes.

I reached the door to what used to be our room. Inhaling through my nose, I turned the knob and pushed the door open.

I didn't even know her name. She was a house mouse, always hanging around, desperate to become someone's ol' lady. She was legal—about the same age as Mercy. And she writhed underneath him, tits bouncing as he drove into her. I traced the word *Cunt* with my eyes, the letters tattooed between her breasts.

Cunt, indeed.

"Yes, fuck, Mercy, yes!" she cheered.

With his back to me, he couldn't see how my lips trembled, how my heart slipped to the floor and shattered. But she saw.

She froze, her pleasure dying on her lips. "Mercy," she warned.

In that instant, I hardened my features. I brushed away my pain, replacing it with a mask. I let him see me, uncaring, dead soul. I lifted my chin, eyes meeting his, my hard face telling him without words.

It was over.

Then I turned and fled, taking my daughter with me.

It was the last time I saw him.

23

NOW

Mercy

I lie in Claudine's guest bedroom without sleeping, eyes growing sandpaper scratchy from watching the shadows move across the ceiling. I can't sleep even if my mind settled enough. Hot pain sears in my joints, keeping my heart awake and pounding.

It's fitting that my search ends here, in Claudine's bed. Well, not her bed exactly, but still. Over the past twenty years, I've asked myself a million times what might've been if I'd made a different choice. If I hadn't sat at the bar throwing back whiskey. If I hadn't gone up to my old room with the first woman I crossed paths with. Maybe I wouldn't have sent Bree running.

I sigh. It's all in the past. In the morning, I'll get on the Softail and ride back to Connecticut. Salvage what I can, if anything of my old life can be salvaged.

Probably not.

I flex my ankles, point my toes, clench and unclench my fists. A storm must be coming in, because I'm getting stiffer with every moment. Or maybe twenty years of angry inmates' beatings are catching up to me.

No one likes a pedophile.

When I wrote and signed that confession, I committed to twenty years of hell. I'd do it all again. It was worth it. Knowing that Olivia and Cliff got the happy ending I never had was worth it. Keeping my club alive was worth it. I can die in peace.

If only I could will my own heart to stop beating.

The sun sinks into the horizon, the night a deep velvet blue. I turn on my side, inhaling the pillow, pretend it still smells like her. Pretend she never left.

Pretend I never left her first.

I may have my peace, but I'll never lose my regrets. Sometimes one can't exist without the other.

I lie on my left side, the pain in my right hip splitting, searing. If someone were to x-ray it, they'd probably find split bone, everything that I am seeping out of the marrow.

I don't know what I'll find when I return. I don't want to be President. Ravage has done a better job than I ever could. I'll take my place wherever he wants me.

I close my eyes, faces swinging through my vision on a carousel. The River Reapers who left, who became the Bastard Brothers MC. Bastard in high school, his choices still unmade, the monster still unveiled. Bree, that first day we met, her face tipped up toward the winter sun, determination etched in her eyes.

"What are you, twelve?" I murmur, half awake, half buried in the memory.

"More like thirty-five," she whispers from beside me.

My eyes fly open. The tip of her nose is only inches from mine, her hazel eyes bright in the dark. I blink, waiting for the dream to fade.

She doesn't.

"Hi," she says.

I sift through the past few hours, calculating how much I've smoked, summing up just how high I am.

She stretches out a hand, running her fingers along the stubble on my face. "I'm real."

"Ha," I choke out. Maybe I've died. Maybe Beer Can put a hallucinogen in my saddlebag. Maybe Claudine slipped something into my dinner. Because there's no way she's really here.

This version of Bree looks like my Bree, except there are more lines around her eyes, more dark circles. She's skinnier, too. But in her eyes, the spark I always loved is still there.

She touches the gray of my beard. "You look good."

"Definitely dreaming," I murmur. I've seen my reflection. I turn onto my other side, onto my bad hip. Grunting, I shift my weight, rolling onto my stomach. I'm never going to get any sleep. Tomorrow's ride is going to be hell.

"I'm right here," she says, running her fingers through my hair.

I'm cracking up. I've got to be. I thought I could let her go, but I'm not strong enough. I'm delirious and delusional, my mind making up an alternate version so that my broken heart doesn't kill me. Some kind of self-preserving act.

Her hands move the sheets aside. She twists off the lid of the jar. The scent of camphor spreads through the room, awakening my senses. Her hands massage the salve into my hip, drawing blood to the surface of my skin, bringing oxygen into the joint.

It's a really, really good dream.

"Turn over," she whispers. "Let me get at those knees."

"Sure," I grunt. "Why not?" I flop onto my back, tucking my arms underneath my head. "Have at it."

She tugs my jeans down, tossing them onto the floor. A moment later, her hands massage the balm into my knees, the friction warming the joints, assisting the salve.

"Feels real," I murmur.

She shakes her head at me. "You're wide awake."

"You told me to go fuck myself."

"I did," she replies, rubbing balm into my other hip. "I went all the way to the airport, too."

"Airport. Right." My lids slip over my eyes, so heavy. I fight to keep the dream, to see it through to a better ending than the one I got in real life. But I'm so tired, and the balm is already working, easing away the pain.

"I lost your ring," she whispers, "and it made me realize I can't lose you, too."

"Right," I agree. Better to roll with the dream. In real life, Bree would've never hung onto that ring.

"Mercy." She reaches for the nightstand and turns on the lamp. Light floods the room. Picking up my wrist, she lays my hand against her cheek. "I'm really here."

Her skin scorches mine, setting my nerves on fire. I pat the pads of my fingers against her cheek. "Feels real."

She sits looking down at me, shaking her head. "It *is* real."

I stretch my fingers, slipping them into her hair. "Huh." I run my hand through the strands, relishing the silky softness. "How?"

"I took an Uber. You still have that Softail?"

I sit up on my elbows, blinking into the light. "If you're real, how did you get in?"

"Claudine," she says.

"That cunt," we both say.

I grin, then sober. I scoot closer, taking her face in my hands. "I'm so, so sorry."

"So am I."

"I thought . . ." I shake my head. "I didn't think. That was the problem. I felt guilty—about Cliff, about Olivia, about you, about everything—and I let that drive me. I never should've walked out of our house."

She rests her hands on top of mine. "I thought, if I could scare you, you'd reconsider. I didn't think you'd believe me." Tears seep into her lashes.

I wipe them away with my thumbs. "Twenty years." I laugh. "It took twenty years for us to have this conversation."

"We're a couple of stubborn motherfuckers," she agrees, resting her forehead against mine.

"I never stopped," I confess. "The whole time I was inside, you were on my mind. In here." I touch my chest, then hers, laying my hand over her heart.

"I stayed in the house," she says.

"I know."

Her teeth sink into her lip. "I left, sometimes. Shannon or Ravage or Beer Can would stay with Olivia, and I'd go try and wipe it all away."

"I forgive you," I tell her, because I do. I can't blame her for how she's tried to cope. "Will you let me help you heal?"

"I don't even know where to start," she says, "but I want to try. For me. For Olivia. For you—for us."

"For you," I say, cradling the back of her head. "It's got to be for you."

She nods, pressing her lips together. "I wanted to be a family," she whispers.

"We still can be, if you want." My gaze latches onto hers. I'm desperate for her answer, my heart starving.

"I never put in for that divorce," she says, peering into my eyes. "I love you, Mercy."

"I've always loved you, Bree."

And then I do what I should've done twenty years ago.

I tip her chin, angling her lips toward mine. And then I kiss her.

24

NOW

Bree

The second his lips close over mine, a sigh of relief passes through me and into him. I have waited twenty years for this kiss. Twenty years, and it's twenty-thousand times better than I ever could've imagined.

One of his hands curls into my hair, the other falling to my waist. I arch into him, lacing my fingers together behind his neck. My lips open for him, tongue sliding against his, welcoming him into me. He tastes sweet and tangy, with a hint of cool. I slide my lips against his, relishing the way his bigger lips consume mine while giving me oxygen, infusing me with him.

Already I want more.

I slide into his lap, my knees straddling his hips. He presses against me through the sheet, hard and hot even through the worn cotton of my skirt.

"Bree," he says, voice strained, and I can't tell whether it's a plea or an incantation. Maybe both.

I hike the skirt up around my hips. I want to shed every layer between us as fast as possible.

"Bree," he says again, this time with an edge to his voice.

I break away from his lips. "What?" I gasp. I'm impatient, I know. But I don't want to wait another moment.

"Where's—?"

"At work." I seal my lips to his again, then pull away as another thought occurs to me. "Your joints?" I don't want to break the man.

"They're great," he says, his mouth finding mine. He tugs my shirt over my head. It sails through the room, landing on the dresser.

I grin. If I close my eyes, I can pretend we're in the club house. No time has passed. We haven't missed a beat. But I don't need to pretend anymore, because finally, after all these years, we're on the same page.

His hands cup my breasts, palms rubbing against my nipples. Tingles shoot through me, and I press into him, needing more, needing to be closer. If there was a way to break us free from the confines of our bodies and knit every ion of our essences together, I would. And it still wouldn't be enough.

I yank the sheet out from between us, lift my hips just enough to pull my panties down. I wrap my hand around him, his flesh scorching to the touch. There's a fever burning between us, a frantic desire that's been blistering for twenty years.

He reaches between us, fingers slipping against me as he strokes me, pushing me closer and closer to combustion. I shove his hand away, notching his head against me. Then, bringing my lips back to his, I thrust my hips, fitting him into me.

Inch by inch he fills me, pushing up as I slide down onto him. I cry out in relief, in gratitude, thanking the heavens, fate, whatever brought us back together. His hands guide my hips, changing the angle. He reaches deep inside me, hitting the sensitive spot, filling me with both blinding pleasure and pain. He closes his hands around my breasts, kneading them, tugging me over the edge. I put my hands over his, threading our fingers, letting him hit that spot over and over, body shuddering, senses dulling, pooling, bleeding into margins, my vision going dark.

His stomach tightens, my name leaving his lips like a prayer. We collapse into a heap together, legs tangled, skin slick with sweat.

He pulls the comforter over us, wrapping us with warmth. And then, wrapped in each other's arms, we sleep.

I don't dream. I fall into a shadow land, a place where I'm aware of his touch, his breathing, his scent, but the rest of me is in a deep slumber. Every time I wake, he rises with me, our bodies in sync and craving each other.

We've got a lot of time to make up for.

Every time, before we doze off again, he tells me he loves me, and I believe him.

EPILOGUE

NOW

Mercy

In the morning, I borrow the kitchen and cook too much breakfast for just Bree and me. The thought of hundreds more breakfasts like this one makes me smile. She sits in my lap and I feed her bites of bacon and eggs, unable to physically separate. Not just yet.

Soon there's nothing more to do. Our bags are packed—not an impossible task, since there are only two of them. I hold her in my lap, bringing her hand to my lips.

"It's gonna be a long ride," I warn her. "I'm not as young as I used to be." Even as I say the words, I know they're no longer entirely true. My body has aged, but overnight my heart is younger. Lighter. Freer.

"I don't care how long it takes," she says, nuzzling into me. "I just don't know what I'm going to say to her."

"Who?" I ask, even though I think I already know. Olivia.

"I have so much explaining to do." She sighs.

"We'll do it together," I promise.

"What if she hates me?" Her lips tremble.

I run my fingers through her hair. "She won't. You're her mother. Everything you did, you did out of love for her."

She nods, but I see the fear in her eyes. I hope, in time, that pain will ease. Until then, all we can do is fight for our family.

A key jiggles in the lock. Claudine pushes the front door open, grinning when she sees us. "I hope you two didn't wait for me."

"We did," Bree says, hopping off my lap. She crosses the room and throws her arms around the other woman. "Thank you."

Claudine hugs her back, her laugh surprised. "I was just setting things right, that's all." She holds Bree away from her. "Now hit the road. Your little girl is waiting for you."

Taking a deep breath, I stand. I kiss the top of Claudine's head, thanking her one more time. Then I take Bree's hand and walk her outside. I swing her onto the back of the Softail, then get on in front of her.

"You ready?" I shout over the growl of the engine.

"Not at all," she says, "but I can deal, if I've got you with me."

"Let's go deal, then." I kiss her one more time, then face forward.

The End

WHAT TO READ NEXT

The third book in the River Reapers MC series is under way!

In the meantime, catch up with *A Disturbing Prospect* (Book 1) and *A Risky Prospect* (Book 2). Visit **elizabethbaronebooks.com**

Already caught up? Join my reader group to chat with other fans of the series. Visit **bit.ly/BaronesBelles**

ABOUT THE AUTHOR

Elizabeth Barone writes books starring badass belles who chose the other path because her life is just as offbeat. Before publishing her debut novel, she was a chef, web designer, apprentice teacher, and retail soldier, but writing is her first love. It took a debilitating autoimmune disease to make her realize it was time to chase her dream.

Elizabeth is the author of over a dozen contemporary romance and suspense novels. She lives in Connecticut with her real-life book boyfriend (husband) Mike and their feisty little cat Squirt.

Connect with Elizabeth
https://elizabethbaronebooks.com
elizabethbaronebooks@gmail.com

facebook.com/elizabethbaronebooks

instagram.com/elizabethbarone

twitter.com/elizabethbarone

amazon.com/author/elizabethbarone

goodreads.com/elizabethbarone